fragments of a fragmented life

a collection of short stories

dana macy

ƥ
fictionLit Press

=

Copyright © 2016 by Dana Macy

ISBN-13: 978-0692751039

ISBN-10: 0692751033

Available through Amazon Books.

Published by fictionLit Press

Ojai, California

for Kala

who every day, shows me

how to laugh again

"It is time to come to your senses. You are to live and to learn to laugh. You are to learn to listen to the 'verfluchte' radio music of life and to reverence the spirit behind it and to laugh at its distortions. So there you are. More will not be asked of you."

—From *Steppenwolf* by Hermann Hesse

ACKNOWLEDGMENTS

I am forever grateful to the members of the Ojai Writing Workshop for their invaluable critiques and inspiration; and especially for our dedicated guides, Doc and Zoe Murdock, who brought us together over thirteen years ago. For my Ventura writer friends for being the kind of readers that writers dream about. For the spirited members of the Ojai Novel Writers Group (aka, the Blockheads) who have stood by each other over the years. Hans Georg Türstig for fixing my computer in far-away lands, and for his translations of many stories into German. Huge thanks to Mayo Morley at Mayo's WORDWORKS, for her mastery in the world of digital publishing, and expertise in graphic design. And finally, Kala, for the design of the book cover, her encouragement along the way, and her patience when I sought hours of solitude.

CONTENTS

FRAGMENTS

TRANSITION

THE HUMAN CONDITION

INDIA

FRAGMENTS

A D-FLAT-MAJOR 7ᵀᴴ
SORT OF DAY

"Stop, hey! what's that sound, everybody look what's going down."

The earth rumbles in Japan while old tunes play at Starbucks on Oppenheimer Boulevard in Los Alamos, New Mexico. And all is well. But wait a minute, something's off here.

A guy walks in wearing an expensive steel-gray down jacket, snapped up all wrong. A Barbie-doll-like lady in stiletto heels and hot pants on this frosty spring morning is complaining that her macchiato is too strong. And here comes one of Los Alamos' autistic physicists—as in 'Asperger's'. How can I tell?

It's the way he sidles sideways like a scared pony when another human being comes close. He pulls his sleeve over his hand when he opens the door. He's thinking about a possible meltdown in Japan.

A glass crashes to the floor. "Mazel tov!" Someone shouts..." somethn's in the air today.

A few days ago, I flew from Delhi into Harrisburg International Airport. That's in Pennsylvania. The wingtips nearly grazed the cooling towers of Three-Mile Island. I contemplated that this might be an ideal terrorist target. Today I'm safe in Los Alamos, having coffee. From my easy chair I see teleported images of frantic human beings in Japan waving strips of torn bed sheets from rooftops, surrounded by raging waters. Tsunami. I return to my computer where problems of voice, tense and point of view in my story eclipse the story in Japan. I wonder that an espresso here is only twenty-five cents more than an espresso in India.

"Stop! Hey, what's that sound, everybody look what's going down."

ASHES ON THE WIND

I ask you to imagine in your mind's eye, a sparkling blue-green pool where precious little babies splash and laugh, secure in mommy's arms while she sings…

"Ring around the rosy
a pocketful of posies
ashes, ashes
we all fall down!"

Delightful? Yes? No? I'm feeling something else, something I don't want to feel. It's a gasp, a sudden sense of life's brevity. It's sharp like fear and stabs at the gut first and then shoots up to the brain and my brain says no, no to the dark side. Just look at those happy babies. I look and see new life on the breath of destruction.

This pool where the babies swim happens to be in Los Alamos, New Mexico. This is the Secret City, home of The Manhattan Project—home to nuclear waste, to uranium and plutonium caches. Just ten days ago a tree fell on electrical wires and the forest was in flames. The entire town of 11,000 was evacuated. Today the town returns…

"Ring around the rosy …
a pocket full of posies…ashes, ashes…"

Is it only me that sees a smoky irony in all this? Mommies sing and babies laugh and tonight is Trivia Night at Quark's Lounge.

Quarky questions. What do you know?

Lucky Buddha Beer for Six Bucks!

Happy Hour no less. This sort of trivia does not come cheap. Do you think…I mean, that this is all about critical mass?

SMITTY'S CASE

Tattered overalls rode too high on his spindly legs. Hairy legs. Blotched, scabby legs. He clutched a DIACK violin case to his chest,

"Can't take inside!" Smitty's shoulder jerked—"No, not leave outside!"

He'd found the ruined case at the thrift long ago and duct-taped the broken hinges. Since then the violin case held his greatest treasure.

A volunteer clerk held the door open and smiled. "Come in Smitty."

Smitty shuffled to the racks and brushed his hand over a blue and purple paisley shirt.

"That will look nice on you, Smitty." She eyed his too short soiled overalls. "And pants?"

"No pants…I like these."

"You remember where to change?" The clerk handed him a crumpled plastic bag and nodded toward the back room. "That's for your old shirt, Smitty."

There were others waiting. It was their day to change into fresh clothes. All were grateful though they did not know who allowed this kindness.

Outside the door, where pavement led to pavement and cars rushed toward Shangri-La, Smitty set his violin case on a bus stop bench and took out a tarnished flute and began to play.

§§§

We'll never know if Smitty's performance was out of gratitude or simply that he never planned the where and when of anything.

Smitty did not see those who gathered—those who saw the tenderness behind his closed eyes. He did not see those who listened and imagined the story behind the creases of his wearied face. There were those who wondered just what it was that had been so very important moments before this exquisite Chopin transcended past and future. Smitty did not see the tattooed biker whose shoulders shook as he hung his head and wept.

ACCIDENT

It's important that you know, I was in my youth, meaning my early thirties, and that just minutes before the accident, I'd enjoyed a wee toke to stave off a dreary premonition. This happened during the mid '80s, before drivers were assaulted with warnings: Driving high is driving drunk. Such billboards are a dangerous distraction in my opinion, but this was not my problem that night. It was the lights—traffic lights, taillights, headlights, and a full moon that blurred my vision.

Stopped at a light on Divisadero, one of San Francisco's most famous streets, I became mesmerized by the couple in the vehicle ahead as they enjoyed a long kiss. It was sweet and I smiled. The light turned green and the couple drove on. I did not. Metal scraping metal jarred my reverie. Through the rear-view mirror, I watched a woman with grey, kinky hair walk toward me in the fog. With bugged out blue eyes she peered into my window. I was reminded of my mother when she was furious but couldn't decide whether to punish me or not. I rolled the window down.

The woman tilted her head, perplexed: "Whatever were you thinking…backing up on a green light?"

I didn't try to make up a clever story. Truth was, I couldn't talk. The woman was calm when she asked me to get out and look at the damage. Her Beetle was seriously crumpled whereas my Jeep suffered only a smear of yellow paint. Had I confused my automatic Jeep with the manual shifter of my MG?

A slight smile passed on the gray-haired woman's lips and she patted me on the shoulder. "Never mind, I know. Don't worry about it dear…and, be careful, driving high is driving drunk."

CHURCH OF THE DONUT HOLE

She couldn't see much through the hole, but she saw enough for five thirty in the morning. Twyla sat in a fluorescent-lit bakery facing a narrow street, the shop's red neon lights reflected in potholes where black ice froze in the wind. An old Baker Woman shuffled behind steel fixtures that held fresh-baked donuts. Twyla shuddered. This was not her idea of a wholesome breakfast, but today her hunger won out. The donut in a small white bag would have to hold her over until Whole Foods opened.

Still, the donut had possibilities. Twyla examined its shape and tilted the sticky object toward the top of the building across the street. Peering through the donut hole, she saw a dozen or so seagulls perched on the precipice of a dismal building. The gulls stared back at her, their plump white shapes eager against dark storm clouds. Ah, fellow scavengers!

Seagulls are birds in the family Laridae, species of Larus, from the Greek, meaning ravenous sea bird. Twyla could relate. Unlike the gull, she felt a twinge of guilt that she would eat the donut. It went against her principles. She admired the gulls, acrobats of the sky, performing effortless antics, catching wind currents with perfect timing and precision.

These gulls were of the western variety, far from the perceived nuisance most believe. They are sanitation engineers with wings, scavenging up great numbers of dead animals and organic litter that pose a health hazard to humans. Maybe she wouldn't eat the donut. She brushed flakes of sticky glaze from her sleeve and realized she hadn't eaten sugar in ten years. The macadamia-flavored coffee would have to do. She stuffed the donut back into its bag. Later she would throw it away, or maybe she'd give it to the next homeless person that might be crouched in a doorway. She did not want to offend Baker Woman, who was at that moment passing by with crumbs cradled in her apron. Out on the street, she flung bits of cookie crumbs and old donuts on the pavement. Her face was blank and revealed not a hint of expression, no sense that she was doing something good, or bad. She did not look up at the seagulls, but only down, watching her feet as she wobbled back to her shop. Baker Woman hardly seemed present. It was as if she'd left her body back in China a century ago, an old woman squatting beside a fire, stirring rice perhaps.

Pounding metallic music rattled the donut trays but Baker Woman didn't seem to hear. Perhaps she felt the music. She must have chosen this type of music to draw students who came by her shop in droves. Twyla would like to ask Baker Woman if she could hear the music, but the old woman spoke no English. Baker woman gestured, holding up a carton of half and half. Twyla shook her head, signaling a definitive 'no'. Not knowing what more she could possibly communicate, Twyla turned to look out on the icy streets. The seagulls would surely come for the crumbs at any moment.

A young man on a bicycle peddled through the pile of breadcrumbs, scattering them in all directions. He smiled as if he got great pleasure in doing this. Twyla smiled too. Hell, that was her on a bicycle just ten years ago, bright-eyed and bushy-tailed—wouldn't be caught dead eating in a donut shop. Back then she was all about saving the planet. Her goal was to achieve an invisible carbon footprint.

Twyla wondered if Bicycle Man rode in this wretched thirty-degree weather to an early class at the local college, passing by the donut shop at the same time every day, scattering Baker Woman's bread crumbs for the seagulls that would swoop down and devour the broken pieces. Twyla imagined that he took pleasure in knowing that this would make Baker Woman smile, for certainly she threw the breadcrumbs from her apron at the same time every morning.

Baker Woman stood behind the counter arranging donuts. Glazed and unglazed, chocolate-covered donuts, jelly and crème-filled donuts.

Twyla watched Baker Woman's withered face for signs of life. What was that? A flicker on one side of her face, an effort to smile. Perhaps she was remembering her youth? Perhaps riding her bicycle with her sister on the way to school by the sea, laughing about the silly boys they'd flirted with. The shop door opened with a tinkle of bells that hung above the door. An old woman shuffled in and joined Baker Woman behind the counter. Twyla watched the two women. Sisters perhaps? She walked over to pay for the coffee and donut. Baker Woman stood a bit taller than before, linked arm in arm with the other woman who was wrinkled and toothless and who did speak English.

"You like? Yes? Our baking and coffee?"

Twyla smiled, lowering her head slightly as if to honor them and to say thank you all in one gesture. When she looked up she saw brown eyes gleam with pride, shining like tinsel on a Christmas tree or sparks from fireworks on New Year's Eve.

"Our own shop, my sister and me," the toothless old woman said, her finger wagging back and forth between herself and Baker Woman. "We come all way from China. You are first customer of day. Very lucky we are. And you lucky too. Have a nice day."

BLINDED BY THE LIGHT

I was what you'd call a "seeker of truth," or less complimentary, a girl still looking for herself. After one trip to India and a few ecstatic moments, I thought I'd found my community for life. I felt *special*. Who wouldn't after all—to live in a community of fellow seekers, nestled in the Catskills of upstate New York. Our focus was one, and that was to achieve liberation in this lifetime.

It was the early '80s. Our community was small—nearly five hundred latter-day-hippies who lived in down vests and down booties in order to save electricity. Our recently deceased guru had purchased one of the Catskills resort hotels. Cocktail lounges were converted into meditation halls and hotel rooms into dorms. My room was outfitted with four bunk beds where eight women shared one closet and one bathroom. Eight of us showered, did our hair and dressed each morning to be present for yoga and meditation at precisely 4 AM. We baked fresh bread each day, rode our bicycles through the countryside, skied the trails, and meditated daily. We chanted sacred Sanskrit scriptures morning, noon and night. Chanting was the elixir that bonded us at the deepest level of our being. Every cell in our bodies seemed to vibrate at a higher frequency. And that was special— so special that the necessary trips into the "outside world" felt like an assault on our sensibilities.

During my first summer in the Ashram, we built a small temple of marble and installed a bronze murti, a life-sized statue of our gurus' guru's guru. The eight hundred pound, gilded gold murti, transported from India, was imbued with prana, considered to be the life force. Even the foundation excavation pit was honored with ceremony. Dressed in our best silk, we circumambulated the pit, offering incense, flowers, and sacred remnants of clothing once worn by gurus of the lineage. The temple was surrounded by grand magnolia trees, blooming wisteria and an exquisite rose garden, wafting blessings over our ceremonies. We chanted day and night for seven days. We were ecstatic.

Even as our small community enjoyed this blissful lifestyle, a new plan for our haven was brewing at International Headquarters in India. During the spring of my second year, our newly appointed guru arrived by helicopter. She was a young Indian woman, charismatic and beautiful. She wore flowing red silk gowns and exuded a seductive essence of the finest essential oils. She moved as if floating on clouds and we fell in love with her grace and humor.

As it happened, our idealism, our love for community, and our desperate search for an absolute truth, led us unquestioning into total surrender and devotion to our new guru. Little did we know that our blissful lifestyle was about to change. We were in for a face-lift. Literally. All five hundred of us were packed off in yellow school buses to Paramus Mall in New Jersey, where personally appointed fashion consultants created new wardrobe acquisitions based on our color charts. Women were coached by beauty experts on how to apply make-up, where I learned, by the way, that a touch of rouge on the chin would lend "a cheerful continence." All of this we abhorred. We returned to the ashram dressed in straight skirts with matching jackets and our feet squeezed into pointed-toed pumps—all fit to impress Hollywood celebrities who would soon grace the Ashram's hallowed halls. Twice each year we tripped off in school buses to freshen our appearance. All of this was funded from the Ashrams' donation coffers. Even the meditation hall was decked out with glittering chandeliers. The more we shone, the more the money flowed. Funny how that works. Gradually, we were inducted into the ways of the world. We learned that all we had to do was show up and miracles would manifest by the grace of the guru. And it worked, it really did. We did our seva, our selfless service, from ten to thirteen hours each day. We understood that our ceaseless efforts were powered by the Shakti, the highly-charged energy generated by our spiritual practices. Grand festivals for the never-ending Indian holidays kept us busy decorating, upgrading accommodations, landscaping, and so on. Extravagant programs were designed to draw flocks of devotees from faraway lands. Thanks to the grace of the guru, we had help. Volunteers were recruited from around the world and all felt privileged to be invited to the guru's house. That's what Ashram means by the way. Guru's House.

To the amusement of us all, our guru invented methods to groom us for future challenges. Psychology Ph.D.'s were sent to the fields to pick up rocks. Medical doctors were assigned to clean toilets. There was one occasion where the translation department desperately needed a Russian translator but the only English speaking Russian was sent to do housekeeping seva. Go figure. We'd learned, however, that these absurdities were to be accepted without question. This was about destroying the Ego— one step toward our goal of attaining *enlightenment*.

Some were fortunate enough to ply their trade. Writers wrote the guru's talks and the guru's books. Artists came from around the globe to refurbish statues of Hindu deities that graced the Ashram grounds. Among the many revered deities are Ganesh, the remover of obstacles; Shiva, the Creator and Destroyer of the Universe; and, the Goddess Kali, who's tongue drips with blood and who wears a garland of skulls. She stood larger than life, fierce and poised to destroy the Ego with her arsenal of swords. These statues were painstakingly painted in neon hues of pink, green and blue, and with an abundance of gold trim. These magnificent deities greeted visitors as they arrived and passed through the Ashram's soaring arches, emblazoned with our motto: Tat Tvam Asi. Thou Art That.

We chanted, danced and heard uplifting talks by orange-clad Swamis. We sat cross-legged in awed silence as our guru hypnotized us with her presence.

Our new guru had great aspirations and our community grew. Two years after her arrival, we were two thousand strong, each one of us dedicated to pleasing her. And that we did, thanks to pots and pots of excellent chai. By 5 AM, we hit the ground running. No more time for home-baked bread. Our bicycles and skis lay abandoned and rusting in the basement.

So be it. New experiences were upon us. We discovered that sensuality and spirituality were inseparable. Men and women reported sexual arousal in the presence of the guru. In fact, a heightened sense of desire grew among us like wildfire. As the saying goes, where there's a will there's a way. Deep down we knew our feelings for each other could not be wrong. Despite the forbidden act, we found ways to hook up—in broom closets, inside the steamy greenhouse at night, in dorms under construction, and even in parked cars. We did this under threat of discovery by security guards that roamed the property night and day. But, ahh! The intensity of forbidden love—this was divine.

Our meetups became rampant and our guru rose to the occasion. There was talk of the need to propagate the teachings through fresh new minds that would be born of these matches. Arranged marriages became all the rage. Celibate swamis were charged with the task of organizing singles dances at a nearby resort hotel. And so it was. We trusted and went with the flow. This was looking up!

I did mention arranged marriages, so I must tell you that I, personally, was called to marry an Iranian man who happened to be very wealthy. He was in need of a green card in order to stay in the States and serve the guru. At the Ashram, he was the baker. He and I had always played with our attraction on a purely energetic level. He had a rich uncle in the Hamptons and all was arranged. We would go together for two full months and come to know each other intimately. We would learn to answer immigration questions with experience and facts to back us up. Secretly, I hoped to fall in love. What could possibly go wrong? As our departure date neared, there came a surprise. A swami was sent to inform me that our guru had changed her mind. My man was to join with another woman. No explanation was given.

All things pass, and so it was with the Ashrams' most valuable assets. Sustainability was not part of our "Mission Statement." Arranged marriages failed and the heirs of our tradition were never born. Our numbers dwindled and the future seemed barren indeed. In fact, as barren as the land. You see, our guru's right hand man, a self-proclaimed mercenary from the Middle East embarked upon a heroic effort to please the guru by creating a crystal island in the center of our beautiful lake. Trees were bulldozed, rich soil washed away by rains, fish floated belly up, and silt made its way down river. The subsequent silting of the river delta was traced back to the ashram. Lawsuits were levied. Politicians and environmentalists descended upon us. The ashram was burdened with a legal nightmare. Every devotee attorney was engaged. We began to wonder at the grace of our guru.

Power and greed, egoism, and the devotees themselves brought our haven down. Guru and disciple fed upon each other. That's how it works. As truth seekers with truth-seeking hunger, we blindly believed our charismatic guru. Every word was sacred. We'd been hypnotized and willingly gave up our personal power in exchange for acceptance into the club. This was expected. This was the command of the guru.

Wealthy devotees showered the guru with gifts of houses in France, Italy, Santiago, Hollywood, and expensive cars driven by coifed chauffeurs. Is it surprising with so much adoration and material pleasures that gurus succumb?

Still, we were a community and the bond between us was deep. We were under a spell that seemed impossible to break, and the drama was addicting. However, our days were numbered. Our Ashram as it turned out, was a sum of destructions—aspirations crushed, souls diminished and the natural environment reduced to rubble. What a beautiful and senseless dream—this sacred solution to save ourselves.

GOD'S CLOUD

" Attention all students and teachers. We have just received word that President Kennedy has been shot and killed. We will observe one minute of silence." It was an awkward silence. We looked at the floor, our small, tight sobs sucked up by the thickness of death. A sudden gust of wind cast shadows from a crooked old oak outside the classroom window. What could we understand in that moment, in our fourth-grade minds? I covered my face, not wanting to show that I didn't know what to feel. Pressing my forehead on the marred wooden desk I cried without knowing why. I turned to look at Kate and she looked at me, her blue eyes teary, wetting the carved initials on her desk. K & R—Kate and Rachel. I hurt for Kate more than our president. I could feel her pulse pressing against my heart from across the aisle. We were close, like soul mates as people say these days. President Kennedy was the first grown up person that we knew who'd died. We watched the ceremonies and saw that honoring a person was a good thing.

I've never told a soul about this, but now it's time. At the end of our fourth-grade year we made a pact. We had a hiding place under a spruce with branches that hung to the ground like sweeping green wings that hid us from the world and kept our secrets. It was here that Kate and I made a pact in honor of our friendship.

Kate spread her flannel quilt, sewn from remnants of pajamas that her Grammy made. I brought a candle and matches and Kate brought a sewing needle and Band-Aids. We sat cross-legged facing each other, lit the candle and sterilized the needle in the flame. Kate stuck my pinky and I stuck hers. Our blood seeped out in small beads on the tips of our fingers and we touched them together to mix our blood. Kate kneeled in front of me and pressed her forehead against mine. "Say, until death do us part." Together we said, "Until death do us part." Kate took my hand, holding it over her heart. "You and me, Rachel...we'll always be together even when we die. You'll know what I'm thinking and I'll know what you're thinking...forever, until the end of time." Right then and there she promised me an eternity of love and friendship in an unsafe world.

Most days Kate and I sat on my front porch swing. We sat for hours, tiptoes pushing against the railing to keep the swing going. We'd hook our pinkie fingers together to join our thoughts while we tried to guess what the other was thinking—about a certain book or a certain boy. On cloudy days, we played a game of naming clouds—White Bunny Running, Black Cat Running, The Mashed Potato. When the clouds were big and puffy and piled up on each other we called them God's Cloud and tried to guess what would happen next. All that feels like a dream now.

One summer day, the air was damp and thick with the smell of ozone. Lightning sliced through black clouds against a zinc yellow sky and leaves flapped in a restless wind. Branches of one-hundred-year-old elms formed an arch over our street. On this Sunday, those branches hung heavy with rain and shook when thunder cracked inside black, boiling clouds. A car rolled slowly up the road, plowing furrows through deep puddles. I knew the car, a grey Buick with red leather seats. Kate saw me on the swing and pressed her nose against the foggy window and laughed. It came to me with a chill, that silent laugh from behind the glass. We waved to each other and that's when it happened. Jagged streaks of lightning reflected in the window and Kate's face was lost in the flash. The hundred-year-old elm in my front yard split down the middle and teetered over crumpled metal, muffling screams that stopped as half the tree settled into place. Sirens took up the screaming and like a premonition went silent. Only red and yellow lights revolved, senseless, over the splintered tree and crushed metal. Chainsaws ripped through tree limbs and crowbars pried at car doors. Firemen pulled Kate's parents out first and I could hear them calling for Kate. I heard their calls turn to sobs as Kate's body was placed gently on a cold, unforgiving stretcher. A gloved hand pulled a white sheet over her body. Men in big trucks dragged the heap of metal off the street, scraping the pavement like one last scream. I remember this like it was today. I ran toward Kate but the men held up their hands, signaling me to stop. I screamed at them, my cheeks hot, tears salting my lips. The charred and splintered Elm steamed where the lightning hit. A pile of damp leaves beneath the tree became an instant memorial. An impossible, unbearable memorial. How many times had we raked those leaves into a pile and jumped into the middle, laughing for no reason at all, rolling in red and gold smells, and throwing handfuls of leaves that stuck in our hair. I swore at the fallen tree. It was my tree that killed Kate. I lay in bed for days while a slow-blooming dread crept in the dark. Smells of summer drifted up from the garden, smells that carried memories. Surreal memories.

There was a terrible stillness where Kate once laughed. I hid myself under the branches of the giant Spruce where we'd pricked our fingers and joined our blood, where Kate said we'd be together forever and ever. But that promise didn't come true. She was gone. How could I bear that emptiness?

Over time, the memory of Kate turned to blood inside me and courses through my veins to this very day. Whenever I see lightning, a splintered tree, or smell ozone before a thunderstorm, I remember that day. I think about this--how the sacred and the inane weave a pattern through our lives until in one single moment of chaos, a piece of the sacred disappears forever. All I wanted was to lose myself, to step out of this life, to escape the insanity.

DAMAGE

In winter our house smelled of old wood and the thick odor of an oil-burning furnace. In summer, the scent of blooming lilacs drifted through the house along with clouds of mosquitoes that our mother battled often and liberally with a pump sprayer containing DDT, all the while singing "Que Sera, Sera." She was on drugs. No joke. Little white pills. Uppers we called them.

Angie, Becky and I were fifteen the summer it all started. Racing on Reds was code for our sleepovers. Red was the color of the label on the yellow cardboard box where we found the uppers. My father brought hundreds of pill bottles home from work and stored them in the kitchen pantry. We chose amphetamines and barbiturates—that was speed for our nighttime rendezvous and downers to catch up on sleep—all drugs compliments of drug reps. Back then, telephones were attached to long, curly cords that reached to my bedroom for privacy. I would call

Angie and Angie called Becky and we each called our boyfriends. Our clandestine meet-ups started with a sleepover in my basement. We played pool until my folks went to bed, then we'd sneak to the stable and saddle up Princess and Maya to ride the two miles of country road that separated us from our boyfriends and the warmth of Judge Brown's hayloft. Judge Brown was Charlie's dad and Charlie was my boyfriend. Judge Brown didn't like me because I wasn't Catholic. That's why we met up in the hayloft in the middle of the night.

Riding past the reservoir one night, I remembered back when my brother and I were little and our father took us ice-skating. One year he made a canvas sail for our toboggan. He'd skate behind us, steering the sled so wind filled the sail and off we'd go all the way across the ice until we tumbled into the snowbank, laughing until hot tears flowed down our cheeks. He'd taught us to skate backwards and how to spin in one spot by speeding up and holding our arms tight against our body.

One night after meeting up with our boyfriends, I noticed that Angie's shorts were inside out. Thinking about it made me feel sick. I didn't think any of us did *that*. Years later, I heard about the car accident. I felt bad, like maybe it was my fault. During our Junior year, Angie got pregnant. She quit school and married a guy from a small town not far away. She worked as a waitress and put her husband through medical school. Their five children were home with their dad when Angie died in that car accident. I wondered if she was on pills when it happened? It was then that I remembered my mother singing and dancing around the house with so much energy. After my mother died too young, I figured it out. She'd taken those pills from the yellow cardboard boxes. Just like we did.

EMMA

She said it would be fun if we took turns with each other. The game was to kiss on the lips and feel each other–*down there*. We were in ninth grade and bunked in the same cabin at camp. The year we were all together in third grade, we'd found a patch of moss in the woods. It was Emma's idea that time too. The game was to take off our shorts and sit on the moss and tell what it felt like. We giggled and said things like—wet, soft, green, icky. Our camp counselor had told us that two hundred years ago, Indian girls sat on moss when they came into their moon time. That's how Emma got the idea.

The night she hatched the kissing plan, Emma whispered, "Doran...come to my bunk last." The crickets were so loud I knew we wouldn't hear if our cabin monitor checked in. It made me nervous. Emma said it was too early and not to worry. The night was hot but we hid under our blankets anyway. Emma and I kissed, lips closed, bodies pressed together as if it meant something. She said my skin felt soft and damp like the moss and guided my hand between her thighs. Our fingers interlaced, we touched her soft, wavy hairs. Then I touched my lips to the place where her tanned skin met the white of curved flesh. We hid under the covers till morning. We hid like that for years. I transferred from one college to another, running from trouble until I decided to set my life right. Signing up for Army ROTC made me feel special. At least useful. After all there was a war going on.

It was a cool Sunday on a deserted campus. Bright red and gold leaves drifted from buckeye trees. I gathered buckeyes, cool like moss and smooth like Emma's skin. I remembered how we were all those years ago, her fingers tracing my lips, the feel of her hair on my body. It was then I saw her, just her back but I knew her walk, how her hair swung with each step. I saw that she walked with a man.

"Emma!"

I ran toward her. Not thinking, just running. She turned, her green eyes stone cold. She held up a white-gloved hand as if to say *Stop*! I saw she was dressed for church going, her man in dress uniform with a bar of medals across his chest. I looked down at my shoes, ashamed of my outfit — bell-bottom jeans, scruffy clogs, and a sloppy army jacket. This was all wrong. So wrong!

"Doran…meet Charles, my fiancé. Charles…meet Doran." She flashed her fiancé a sidelong glance. "We haven't seen each other in years."

Emma looked me in the eye, her gaze still cold. Charles gave a nod and managed a faint smile. For a moment, no one spoke.

Emma broke the silence. "We've a lunch engagement. I'm afraid we've got to hurry on. You take care, Doran." Her eyes softened a little before she turned and walked away.

I saw my father not long ago. He told me that he was ready to meet his maker. Then he said, "Doran, I've failed you. God means for us to marry, to procreate, to prosper and take dominion over the Earth." He grimaced. "What did I do wrong?"

I thought of Emma and how I could never tell him. This moment should be honest I thought, but telling would send him to the grave broken and hurting. In the end, I didn't tell.

Outside, the air was crisp with fresh snow. I wandered through a wooded area where a sliver of sun divided light and dark, like the tan line on Emma's back. I lay in the snow looking up at the clouds, remembering how she touched me, how she formed me. She thought of me too. I knew she did.

JUST SAY'N

It's funny that you mention people that make up stories. You say you've been gullible at times; that for several years you lived with a man who you finally figured out was making up the stories he told you. "And his stories weren't even that interesting!"

Well, my friend, I know some people (on dating sites for example), who fabricate an elaborate persona—women pretending to be men to see the women who are their competition. Or, women looking for women (who really aren't looking for women, or maybe they are but don't know it yet). A legitimate form of voyeurism I suppose. At least one with a useful outcome. Potentially.

Dating sites and Facebook have something in common. I'm reminded of the women who sit on display in the veiled windows of Amsterdam's Red Light District—Angels of Compassion they're called. No judgment there. I admit that I pose on Facebook under a fictitious name. What is fiction and what is truth, you might ask. Well…it's complicated. There are hapless wandering souls (God bless them) that construct a grandiose life story. Perhaps one such wanderer imagines that his father was an ambassador to China and was murdered by the Shanghai Green Gang, leaving his family destitute (which would explain why the person is homeless now). I met him on a bus in Boston and he most certainly believed his story. It was true for him.

Here's a story for you. Not one of my fictional stories, but an example of how a mind can confuse fact and fiction. Grad school, Utah State University (circa 1979). My friend Sophie lived an unconventional lifestyle, miles up a remote canyon. She slept in a hammock in a pump house on her boyfriend's land. I wanted to live on the land like she did so the two of us got the idea we'd buy a caboose and haul it up the canyon, fix it up with a wood-burning stove, and live in this caboose. Sherm, Sophie's boyfriend, said we could set it on the concrete pad he'd built for unidentified flying objects that'd never showed up.

Salt Lake City Salvage Yard was our first stop. Behind a chain link fence bordered by tumbleweed and cracked concrete, we found our caboose. The salvage yard guy told us it was ours for $10,000.00. We had cash and told him that we wanted the caboose. He asked how we planned to transport the caboose to Logan (two hours away) and up the canyon. We hadn't thought about that. We were in luck though. The salvage yard guy told us he knew of a transport company that would help us out. The estimate for transport came in at $7,000.00. We abandoned the project.

Twenty-five years later Sophie and I ran into each other at a meditation retreat near Yosemite. We laughed and shared new stories. I asked her, "Did we really look for a caboose to live in up Logan Canyon?" I honestly didn't know if we'd done that or if I'd made it up — perhaps a story I'd thought of writing based on the caboose in the movie, Henry and Maude. Sophie laughed, and said that was all true.

TRANSITION

THE GIFT

The pendant was an unexpected gift, carefully wrapped in a torn off piece of pink Kleenex and placed in a plastic laboratory vial.

The giver of the pendant, whose name was Thomas, and the receiver of the pendant, his lab assistant, whose name was Claire, had often shared small things. They took turns, pressing their eyes against an ocular rubber piece that led to a much bigger world where purple and green dyes revealed circular jelly like shapes. Inside the circular jelly-like shapes, yellow-dyed fragments wiggled their way into X-shapes.

Thomas explained. "Think of it as a peanut butter and jelly sandwich. You put jelly on one side and peanut butter on the other, then slap the two slices together for a second and pull them apart. Some peanut butter gets mixed in with the jelly and some jelly gets mixed in with the peanut butter."

Claire sighed. "Just like that...and here we are without our asking to be."

"Yes, just like that. And it goes on forever."

"Until it ends."

"Yes, until it ends."

Thomas changed the slide. "Now look."

Claire pressed her eyes to the rubber eyepiece. Once orderly and predictable cells had morphed into shapeless globules. Aberrant cells.

On occasion Thomas and Claire would walk from the labs to a nearby cemetery and sit together under a sycamore tree with a view of old marble gravestones. They would open their lunches of peanut butter and jelly sandwiches and eat in silence. With respect for the dead.

One day Thomas broke the silence. "You're wearing a scent...patchouli and vanilla I believe?"

"Pleasant I hope."

"Always. But what I want to tell you, is that at times, I smell a scent and hear a sound, or vice versa."

"Synesthesia. I've heard of it."

"I'll hear a chipmunk chirping and smell honeysuckle."

"It must be confusing...I mean...for a scientist."

"I figure it out. But then there's you."

"What about me?"

"With your scent, I hear strains of Chopin. It's special for me. I will always remember this."

"Hmm." She let that one go and they lapsed into silence.

All of this happened before the pendant was given.

Thomas and Claire once again sat under the sycamore tree with their peanut butter and jelly sandwiches.

"I'd like to tell you a little story, Claire. Bear with me, this happened before you were born."

Claire nodded and gazed into the distance, over the gravestones. "Sure."

Thomas took a deep breath and let it out again. "I was wrestling for sport in Beijing. It was the beginning of Operation Desert Shield, when the US and China were coming to terms, over mutual economic advantages of course. One day a man by the name of Li Qiang walked into the ring and challenged me to a match. Li Qiang was a Communist, but no matter, we became friends. Willing combatants, you might say."

"During one such match, exhausted, arms and legs entwined, I smelled his sweat mingling with my sweat… and I heard strains of Chopin."

"Hmm." Claire had no other comment. Thomas' stories were always complicated.

"My first thought was of Tiananmen Square. A student sang Chopin's Funeral March, just the year before. Odd isn't it? This has nothing to do with death you understand, but when I smell your patchouli and vanilla, I remember Li Qiang. There was something sweet about our friendship, Li Qiang and I. We both felt this. We saw it in each other's eyes, but we never spoke of it. On parting, he gifted me a gold pendant. A Chinese character filled the center of the pendant. Li Qiang traced the lines of the symbol with his finger, and whispered … "Longevity.""

"So, this is about death, isn't it … longevity or death … like the cells under the scope."

Now it was Thomas' turn to wonder. "Hmm…one never knows." Thomas reached into the pocket of his lab coat. "I want to give you this—because of your scent, and his scent, and Chopin. You're leaving soon and I want you to remember me, just as I remember Li Qiang."

Claire did leave and never returned. Years later, word came that Thomas' body was riddled with cancer. Claire retrieved the gold pendant from a box containing precious gifts she'd received over the years. As her finger traced the lines of the Chinese character, she heard strains of Chopin.

FREEFALL

You had a talent for escaping the ordinary, like the time your parachute didn't open. Instead of crasning to your death, a voice entered your head. That's what you told me, a voice came into your head and changed your destiny.

Yes, a voice willed me to pull the ropes with all my strength. I obeyed. I thought nothing. I felt nothing. My life did not flash before me. In the last seconds, two pockets bloomed and broke my fall. The fresh-plowed dirt of a cornfield was soft and forgiving. My body fell limp, head caught in the risers, eyes fixed on the sky. It took years to understand.

Years later…

We meet again. What are the chances? Last I heard you were falling through space, headed for a shallow grave.

So, you remember my story? Back then I thought I'd been spared for a reason, that a higher calling awaited and my life might be somehow…well…enlightened, that I might escape the traps of this life. Now I tell you that nothing has changed.

How has nothing changed may I ask?

It's a riddle you know. We were between youth and adult and we played like children without a care. We fell and stood up, and laughed at our foibles. One day we looked around and saw that years had passed. Here was another world and it was serious business. We shed tears and tears became pools and pools became oceans. Dams broke and we slipped and fell into a dream. We drowned with the masses—such a strange beast. Vicious. Insidious. Our hearts beat wildly. We saw ourselves for what we are, mere homunculus blobs in freefall. There were moments when the sun caught us cheering like children sliding down an icy hill. Torments followed thrills and we asked, why am I here? God, please don't let me make this mistake again. God answered and grace descended upon us. We awoke, grasping for the joy of our child life. We smiled for no reason at all and went for the freefall. We played our parts and it was beautiful. We were born again with fresh eyes. A sense of oneness was within our grasp. Even the relentless din of humanity was a beautiful thing. We thought we'd found meaning after all, until we fell into the dream once again. We dreamed over and over again and on waking we asked, what am I doing here?

What is this dream? There were no answers, no escape and we came to know the meaning of surrender. Our dreams became playgrounds where we watched our children grow. We watched them fall and cry our unshed tears. They dreamed this life all over again. We watched and blessed them, willing meaning and love into their lives.

ONE CHRISTMAS FAR AWAY

What we saw seemed like a dream. Our eyes and mouths open wide, not believing the spectacle in the sky. Every one of us silent. Someone had jumped from an airplane and floated to the beach where we stood. As the jumper came closer, we saw that it was a man. We saw that he was very fat and wore a bright red suit with a black, shiny belt around his tummy. His white beard was the bushiest and the longest that I'd ever seen. Santa Claus landed on the beach and his rainbow-colored parachute collapsed in the sand at our feet. My brother nudged me and I knew he'd noticed too—that Santa's big nose looked familiar.

It was 1963. My brother and I stood barefoot on a sugar-white beach with a small group of kids from a Florida orphanage, all of us around six years old or so.

The orphans could sit on Santa's lap before my brother

and me. After all, we were only silly northerners who arrived on Sanibel Island every Christmas to have a picnic on a deserted beach, eat oranges and dip our toes in the too-cold water.

Nearly sixty years later, on Christmas Day, our Papa passed away. The memorial was traumatic for me. I was called upon to speak at the one room stone church that stood in the middle of our family cemetery. The mourners sat in worn wooden pews and consisted of an aunt and uncle, both over ninety years old, and two cousins I'd played with as a kid. I was the first to stand up and tell how great a man my Papa had been. My hands shook but I managed to read the words I'd written on the page.

I can only tell you how I remember my Papa. How in winter he made a sail of canvas and attached it to our sled. How we caught the wind and sailed clear across a sea of ice as Papa skated behind us, forward and backwards and in circles, reaching the other side before we hit the bank. How he made turtle soup from the big ones that crawled up the riverbank. How he taught us to dress out a rabbit for dinner and make mittens from multi-colored pelts. How he taught us to slit a chicken's throat and boil it in a tub over an open fire. How he always said, "You never know when you'll need these skills." How, for Christmas he gave me books on *How to Raise Goats*, and later in life, how his gifts were always *Do-It-Yourself Manuals*. How he taught me to splint a broken finger with a Popsicle stick and duct tape. How to tie a square knot and pound nails. How he loved his parakeets and named them all Pepper. How he taught us to make wine from Concord grapes and how there was always an inch of sludge at the bottom of the bottle. How he moved me from apartment to apartment, from broken heart to broken heart. How he was always there for me. How Papa grew old and gaunt and thin.

It was on Christmas Eve, the eve of his death, that I held his hand and asked, "Do you remember the time you parachuted from a plane and landed on Sanibel Island? How the orphanage kids climbed up on your knee, their eyes big and unbelieving? How they played with your beard. How you gave them peppermint candy canes and presents?"

He turned his head to look at me and I imagined that he almost smiled…that I saw a faint glimmer in his eye.

NOWHERE TO FALL

A figure lay still and silent, like a fallen angel, a fragile beauty on concrete. Stunning in a morbid sort of way. The body was a female human, albino-like in white tights and a sleek faux fur jacket to match. Ebony cheeks glistened like silver moons. Her sea-green eye shadow became sticky in the drizzling rain and sealed her eyes shut. Her body formed an 'X' on the damp concrete sidewalk. Purple and green marquee lights swept over her body. She did not move and she felt nothing.

Nearby a crowd gathered, bending to peer into a wire cage. A benevolent white rat perched comfortably on the back of a black cat. Both the cat and the rat snuggled marsupial-like with an unidentified breed of dog whose body was shaved smooth from head to tail. These creatures licked and groomed each other and if you watched closely you could see them exchange soulful glances.

Passersby laughed and walked around the body. Some took photos of X-Girl thinking she was an act like all the others. X-Girl became soggy and smeared like a forgotten chalk message. A man in black stood watching, a cigarette dangling from grey lips. He watched as a puddle formed around X-Girl's head, the red of it trickling through neon reflections and into the muck of the street.

With a sigh, the man in black tossed a nicotine stub into a puddle and shuffled closer. He knelt beside her and whispered in her ear, "…remember when you were a child playing?"

X-Girl heard this and remembered such a time. Her voice was faint and the man leaned closer.

"I'm climbing high in a cherry tree, wearing my favorite cowgirl shirt—sky blue with white trim and pearl snaps."

The man sat with her as she took her last breath and slipped away with a smile on her lips.

OUT OF THE DEAD CITY

I feel like a sparrow, perched in the fenestra of a crumbling 13th century castle in ruins, my purple-splayed feet knowing this place, the ground soggy with the blood of my sisters, strewn about, mouths raw and gaping wide. There are heavy stone steps overgrown with wild mustard. As I climb my legs become heavy and weak. I reach a rusted gate, adorned with seven stars that shine like diamonds. My gut remembers soldiers, the screams of women. And blood. A beneficent white cobra with ruby-red and piercing eyes greets me. "Come, I've been waiting for you…a long time waiting."

Cobra leads me into the courtyard. There I see luminous bodies like shattered crystal lying face down, all heads turned to the right, eyes gazing toward the east as if waiting for the coming dawn. Each body has the shape of a woman.

Blood-soaked soil tells for the hundredth time about the dead with open eyes. I shiver as the moon sinks beyond a stone window—a window that has seen the horrid prosecutions and heard the screams of women, a window where each scream is etched for eternity.

I am not afraid of this place. I am not afraid of the great white cobra when he flares his hood and wills me to mount. Cobra gathers up the dead, landing them on his back where they dangle and sway as we snake through a labyrinth. Fern-like tendrils, vibrant and aware, reach out through cracks in the walls, observing our movement.

We are between life and death, or perhaps we are between death and life. Reaching the center of the labyrinth, a pyramid of jewels stands—unclaimed diamonds, rubies, and amethysts glitter in the moonlight. The jewels begin to vibrate. I reach out to touch a ruby and in that moment the dead awaken. Shattered bodies become whole, skin translucent like milk glass so I can see their hearts beat. The awakened hum softly. Still they don't notice me and I realize I'm invisible to them. Great White Cobra writhes as he carries us back through the labyrinth, arriving once again at the courtyard. The awakened lie down and gaze toward the heavens, open eyes reflecting the moon.

But…I've forgotten part of this dream. Upon entering the gate, I recognized one of the dead. It was me, and in that moment, I sat straight up as if struck by lightning, eyes wide open with wonder. A great 'Ahh' escaped from my soul. It was then that I became invisible and yet I did not know this.

In the end the awakened return to the gate of seven stars. A magnificent "Aum" arose from our throats and we became as one—a great white dove that flew toward the heavens.

THIRTEEN DAYS OF NO

"Eat Mum. It's potato, your favorite…come on now."

"No!"

Her tired eyes squinted through shiny chrome bed rails, "I love you."

"I love you too Mum. Eat some potato."

"No!"

Crowding the hall just outside her door are the chatty night nurses, and there's the too-red lipstick on Nurse Keryn who meets my gaze and nods in that ever-so-compassionate way, meaning, it will all be over by morning.

Mum's last words were a strained whisper, "I eat potato."

I wonder if Nurse Keryn heard her.

DEATH WAS COMING
FOR HER

My friend had always been a difficult curmudgeon. She minced no words. Not on any subject or about any person. That's how she was, until the surgery. The diagnosis was brain cancer. The surgery went well and my friend returned home, determined to beat the cancer. It was then that we noticed a change in her demeanor. She rested on the sofa, not interested in basketball games or her favorite television series, or the books she loved to read. She seemed content and spoke well of people, even those she'd come to blows with over the years. She told us how grateful she was that these people were in her life. She joked that the surgery had left a space in her head and that we all needed more space in our heads. She laughed.

We exchanged mystified glances. This change made no sense. Out of hearing range, we considered the possibility that she knew she was dying and was turning over a new leaf at the very last moment, or, that she was playing with us and getting a kick out of it. But no, she talked sincerely about beating the cancer and of plans for the future. We pondered on this. Here was our friend who'd become another person. Was it possible that brain surgery had rearranged the wiring up there? Or was it a 'consciousness' thing? Did the subconscious know that death was coming and the conscious part of the brain not know?

Our friend once published a collection of poetry and quoted Carl Jung:

"The opposite of profound is silly."

She wrote:

Sing to me, song to me
running to run
canoe to the moon
to the sun, to the sun
Paddle me, puddle
My porridge is cold
We grow younger each year
We grow old, we grow old

The afternoon of her death, she'd been excited about going to a deli for a 'build your own sandwich.' At home with the sandwich, before the first bite, she was gone.

ECLIPSE

We took it in the mountains

those unsavory mushrooms, dry and crumbly,

hard to swallow

lying naked expecting nothing and everything

we entered a temple, a vast emptiness

where thoughts of I, thoughts of us,

pain, sadness, happiness, joy

vanished

all movement

all doing

all non-doing

a perfectly choreographed dance

outside of space and time

only the dance remains.

And so it happens —

contraction leads to expansion

and expansion leads to contraction.

Return to mind is painful

other-ness unbearable

We are not the same and

 will never be the same again.

There is a crack in our consciousness that over time

grows into a cave known as

the cave of the heart

where there lives a longing

to go back

from where we came.

THE HUMAN CONDITION

THE NEVER-ENDING 'I'

The universe is not funny, it's fuck'n hilarious! I want you, she wants you, and you want him. Does anyone really want what they can have? My native state is wanting, yes everything and nothing. Can you give me that? Not your life, but give me your desire completely (mind the strain on your conscience).

So, you can only imagine that it will end badly? Doesn't it all? (The clouds portend stormy weather, unusual here where the sun always shines. Here comes one in the shape of a porpoise—or torpedo, or a penis). There it is you say, desire in its one true form—its measure is a life, somewhere a life, and its shape is your very own mind.

She waits on a red bed dressed in moonlight for the one who will not come, for the one not allowing. A warm breeze touches her still innocent flesh where pert little goose bumps melt into dreams, her hips pressing lightly down. Beyond the shimmering curtains are brown mushrooms with pink ruffled edges, pressing up through the wet earth, reaching for a kiss, wanting to be known.

Wait just a minute, you say. Rumi speaks about a

transcendent love, something greater than the small self, not this mundane human desire with the groaning and grinding of sweaty body upon sweaty body, followed by endless compromises, turning lives into sentimental prisons. But, I ask you, what difference if you are sentimental about a god idea or sentimental about a human idea? You won't get past the mind. The mind—always grasping for something, wanting to believe in something, wanting to limit the limitless just to feel comfortable, that is, to find a niche, to fit life into this concept or that concept.

I can't bear it anymore. I want to burn it out totally. Can it be done…if I become desire itself? Deep inside there is an echo. You are already That. Yes! We must be to exist. Damn! There's no escape. This is all there is. I'm sure of it now. This disaster is all that there is. What a relief!

I feel your heart pounding from the next room. The walls are thin here, so thin that I feel you pressing me against your will. You come closer, then stop. You stop over and over again. Tell me, where will desire go? You are vanity itself, to think your desire even matters. How can it matter? Desire will always be. It will never give us up. Immortality exists only in the wanting. It is the never ending 'I', the folly of hope that expresses forever. It is nothing.

So, will you be human? Will you be? She sinks into the fading moonlight on the red bed, the mover of lips, large soft moist ones, made for embracing pleasure and for shaping desire, a limber tongue, sipping the pause waiting for you to come, to open her lips. Imagine such a being. Imagine no end, and let us begin.

FIVE HUNDRED LIGHT YEARS AWAY

A ONE-ACT PLAY

Celaeno [sa-lee-no]

(Narrator reads in playful tone)

Celaeno, not the brightest of the seven sisters, wandered far from Pleiades looking for water. Her star anemone was withering and turning brown. She'd heard about the curse—an abomination from the land called 'Dreaming Dinosaur'. The curse was a sort of totem and wielded an evil power over life forms. Those that once shone with brilliant blue luster withered into dull, non-colored things, and began to stink. Celaeno took flight, heading for the closest shining star. She is drawn to the one with the sword. She remembers a forest, musky and lush. Here she would find the cure for her wilting flower. The healing milk of the galaxy was told to run in rivulets along the engravings of the golden rod. Arriving, Celaeno delights in the thousand hues of gold that glitter beneath her star steps along the labyrinth. And then…

Celaeno:

Oh! My dear neighbor, Orion! What a surprise! Why are you running in the labyrinth?

Orion:

I must check on the point of my sword. The Dreaming Dinosaur is heaving and moaning in her bed. Heaven help us should she awake from the dream. I must stand vigilant and protect our galaxy from the curse.

Celaeno:

Why worry, Orion, the moron Dreaming Dinosaur can never reach us with their evil totems—we are five hundred light years in the future.

Orion:

Ah, but you are wrong, little one. I can already smell their vile thoughts, even more powerful than the totem. They reek of lust and greed and they intend to infect us with their barbaric egos.

Celaeno (distressed)

But how can you save us? Oh Orion, I am frightened! Already my flower is wilting. Has the Dreaming Dinosaur already entered me? I must find the healing flows. Oh! Orion, help me.

Orion: (with bravado)

My dear Celaeno, I will steal light from the sun and blind them. With my sword I will slice a rip in the sky and fill it with the sweet spice.

Celaeno:

Yes! I see it now. Their fat totems of steel will explode in the rip. But first we must search for the sweet spice Orion, you know how the Dreaming Dinosaur loves it. Remember how they swallowed the sun, mistaking it for a sweet fruit?

Orion:

Yes! We saw the fire from here. It burned in their bellies until there was nothing but ashes.

Celaeno: (now serious)

And then we heard the terrible cries of the sea, forced to swallow the gray dust…But what happened next? (holding her head) I cannot remember.

Orion: (sweetly)

My dear little Celaeno, you were young so we hid your eyes. What happened next was only the beginning of the nightmare.

Celaeno:

Oh, tell me… I am fully a woman now. I can take it.

Orion:

I hesitate to poison you, my little flower. But, if you insist. (Orion pauses, gazing into distance) The blue luster had died and lay there weeping in vain…or we could say…that her vanity was weeping. It was her tragic destiny. (Orion hangs his head)

Celaeno: (pleading)

Oh, but you digress, Orion. What happened next, I beg you tell… but hold me, Orion, I am afraid.

Orion:

My dear little Celaeno. I feel your shivering skin and your wilting flower. I fear the evil has already entered you. You may be infected. I dare not tell more.

Celaeno: (beats on Orion's chest)

You will tell me or I will not help you find the sweet spice. It is my sweet spice to give or not to give.

Orion: (feigns irritation)

This is another bribe of yours, little Celaeno, but if you insist. (Orion gestures toward space)

It was like this: The seas roared in agony, forcing the gray dust of the Dreaming Dinosaur down to its depths. It was burning still and caused a fierce churning of the waters. It was horrible.

Celaeno: (Orion holds Celaeno's head to his chest)

That's when we covered your eyes.

Celaeno: (angry, she pushes him away)

But still you cover my eyes! Do you want the sweet spice or do you not, Orion?

Orion: (groans)

You know that I need you. I cannot save our galaxy without the sweet spice to fill the rip.

(Orion groans again)

A premonition grips me, my sweet Celaeno. I fear for your very life.

Celaeno: (coy, pleading)

And yet, my own belly is on fire waiting for you. I beg you, Orion, what did happen? My heart is paralyzed unless you speak. Oh, Orion, my loins ache, awaiting your answer.

Orion:

Oh my little flower, I cannot resist when you talk like that. I'll tell you then. The oceans were filled with suffering and desperate cries rose from gaping mouths. The fire of ambition would not be drowned and erupted from those hapless souls that lingered in want. The fires were miles high and when they cooled. Do you see now why it is called The Dreaming Dinosaur?

Celaeno:

It is foul and ugly. We must find the sweet spice and save our galaxy. Come with me, my dear Orion. My flower knows the way. (She takes his hand and they drift away)

(Narrator reads in solemn voice)

Unfortunately, we have heard in Star News Today, that Celaeno and Orion became lost in the labyrinth of his sword. They were last seen in a cave filled with bluish light. The healing flows seeped from the mouth of the cave where surges of ecstasy were detected. It is thought that the star couplings are slowly drowning in sublime illusions.

IF ONLY I BELIEVED IN SIN

My place around the family table was opposite my father and a painting of Jesus that hung on the wall behind him. It's something I can't explain, but between Christ and my father I was suffocating, and it wasn't Jesus' fault. My father kept saying how Jesus would always be with us on earth and in heaven too, but only if we were good enough to go to heaven. It was then and there, as a Midwestern-born girl child of nine, that true hell seeped into my being. I knew deep down that I'd never be good enough. More than that, I knew that in my soul that I didn't want to be that kind of good.

It was a grey-lit Sunday morning. Anti-war protests were in the news. In New York City WWII veterans staged a rally to protest US involvement in Vietnam. We watched as thousands of draftees burned draft papers. This frightened me. Armageddon was happening! Just like we'd heard in Sunday School. Father lectured as usual, stabbing the air with a chunk of pork roast on his fork. "See that… we need rules. Without rules, there's chaos and lying!" He looked straight into my eyes, the veins in his neck bulging blue and red. "Better believe it…stealing, cheating, wars. You can't have a world at peace…or a town, or a family for that matter, that works without rules. Everyone must obey the rules!" I began to shake. A pea rolled off my fork and into my lap. Rage broiled in my gut and turned into a scream that stuck in my throat. As if war was a game played according to rules! Three of my cousins were in Vietnam. Cousin Chris came home messed up on drugs and shot himself at our family reunion. In front of everybody. So much for your beloved rules! I wanted to scream, but to speak out would mean a whipping. Father's number one rule was that children should be seen and not heard. Do you know what I said about that? Fuck that! Double fuck that! Not out loud of course. In that moment, a rebellious soul was born. I lied. I schemed. I kept secrets. You know, the things we can't tell our families, the secrets we hide for years and are ashamed of, until we just need to tell someone, to atone, to feel better about ourselves. There was the day I took my little brother to the library and showed him pictures of vaginas and penises. I ripped the pictures out and stuffed them in my bib overalls. I wanted to be bad—as bad as my parents were.

What they did one Sunday was unthinkable. It's funny how people judge. It's human nature I suppose. For me it all began with churchgoers. Back then my folks were Christian. So were Timmy's parents. Timmy was my sort-of-boyfriend in fourth grade. Most Sundays our families got together for a picnic at my house. There was plenty for kids to do—a Merry-Go-Round, monkey bars, tire swings and a huge sandbox. Once we snuck into the barn attic, risking our lives on rickety wooden steps that could break through if we weren't careful. Cobwebs and thick dust hung in the air. Hidden beneath old blankets we found Wells Fargo trunks from pioneer days, packed with ladies' nightgowns and baby clothes, yellowed and fragile. A single baby shoe lay in the folds. I touched the cracked leather and thought about pioneers that made it all the way to Ohio, and how they might have died with flu or measles. Or Indian arrows. You think you're having a normal day, until you see these things. Down the barn steps, out in the light of day, was our green lawn with beds of roses and peonies and my tree house. This is another world, one hundred years in the future where our mothers laid out red and white checked tablecloths on the lawn and my father juiced apples right off the tree. Like I said, it's a normal day. Then something happens. Something that makes you feel rotten inside, something that turns your world upside down. You just don't know that it's happening.

On one of these apple-pie–and-everything-wholesome Sundays, a soft ball smashed Timmy's pinkie finger. He rolled on the ground screaming. "I'm gonna die, I'm gonna die!"

What a baby! Still I was scared. I imagined the worst. Maybe he'd pass out, go into a coma and maybe really die. Or, he'd be brain-damaged for life. I searched everywhere but my father wasn't around. None of our parents were around. Finally, I dared to look where we were strictly forbidden. Our house was a three-story Victorian. Six-foot-wide doors pulled out of the wall with little brass pull rings. When these doors are closed there's a crack where they come together. The last place I thought to look was my folks' bedroom. When I saw that these doors were closed, I froze. They were never closed during the day. My parents' bed stood directly in front of my peeping place. I held my breath until my head got light. I was sure that I saw what I thought I saw. No mistake. I ran outside and puked in my mother's Petunias.

You see, Timmy's mom was short and squat with tomato-red hair that looked like she'd been electrocuted. Pale white too. The kids all made fun of Timmy's dad, his hair parted too far down the side and thin, oily strands slicked over the top of his head. The pockets of his yellowish-white shirts bore red and blue ink stains. On the other hand, my mother…she was beautiful. She had long blonde hair and dark blue eyes like Queen Guinevere. My father was tall and smart looking with a full head of curly dark hair and shining hazel eyes. You get the picture. There they were, the four of them, mixed up in my folk's bed. What I saw just wasn't Christian. I saw how rules could bend. I judged.

I remember this now, from a dark place deep inside. I see their bedroom on Sunday mornings as my parents dressed for church, my mother dabbing her favorite perfume, some cheap orange blossom stuff from a tourist trap in Florida. She did that with her ring finger, her wedding ring flashing in the mirror. And there's my father, dressed in his white, starched shirts with silver cufflinks. When I was old enough, he taught me how to make a tie knot and fasten the long and short ends with his diamond tie tack. After he died, I came across that tie tack and wore it as a pierced earring. I never took it out, until I thought…maybe this small diamond held these terrible memories. I tried to take it out, but it was fused to the backing. It had to be cut out.

MIRAGE

On full moon nights in winter my father would open my bedroom door a crack, "Wake up! Let's go!" In minutes, I'd be dressed and follow him down the path to the stables. My snowsuit was sky blue and my boots were the same chestnut color of my pony. I'd named her Maya. My-ya. The syllables felt soft like a secret. On Maya's back I felt free in a quiet sort of way, free on the inside. I smile now, remembering how snow crunched with each step on our way to the barn. How crisp, cold air mixed with smells of the stable, hay, leather, and horse dung—familiar like old friends.

Riding over snow packed country roads under a full moon, my father pointed out constellations and told mythological tales like the one about the Seven Sisters of Pleiades who were mountain nymphs and hunted by the giant Orion for his pleasure. This sounded like a great adventure. I imagined that some night I'd wake up as a nymph and be spirited away to chase around the heavens, playing a game with my sisters and Orion, and I would be the leader whose name was Electra, the brightest star of the Seven Sisters.

This dream followed me on every ride, until one night. From the rail of a wooden fence, my father scooped pure white snow in his bare hand. Snow crystals glittered in the moonlight and he held the mound of snow close to my eyes. "It's beautiful, isn't it?" His voice sounded too serious for such a pretty moment. He was quiet, watching the snow melt and trickle through his fingers. I got shivers and goosebumps even inside my snowsuit. "It's a mirage, he said, it melts away."

We stood in the silence that snow makes, and even Maya inhaled too hard and shook her chestnut mane. My father lifted my chin with his still damp hand. "That's what beauty is…a mirage…remember that. It's pretty but it doesn't last. Someday you'll understand…someday when you look death in the face."

The memory of that night haunts me—the way it started out so happy and then turned so dark. My father showed me that nothing was what it seemed to be, and I became afraid of my dreams.

THE VOYEUR

A scream cut through the hot Berlin night. Then silence. The Professor stood at the fifth-floor window of his flat, looking in the window across the street. He saw nothing at first. A waning moon hung over the deserted street casting a sheer bluish light. Ah there she was! A television flashed anxious and violent in a dark room. A naked woman lying alone, stared blankly through blue flashes. But who screamed?

He turned his focused his telescope. The woman wore a jade medallion that hung between her breasts. She fondled the stone, playing its smoothness over her nipples. He watched as his thoughts wandered to one of his patients, a young woman whose profound absorption with global human conditions was hopelessly confused with her personal reality. The Berlin Wall had fallen, strewing emotional casualties across the country like rubble, and she was one of them.

His hand trembled as he pressed 'play' on his recorder. She was naïve, innocent. "It's the nuclear family I don't understand. Our human duty goes beyond this...and it should, for the greater good."

The Professor's gaze fell. This poignant striving for a moral kind of justice only deepened his agony, an isolation from humanity that left him groping for meaning, searching for a truth that lies beyond justice.

 He focused his camera on the naked woman. He imagined her tender touch as she pressed her hands between her pale, smooth thighs. He took the first shots just as the door of her flat flew open. A surly figure strode toward her. He straddled her, jerking the string of the medallion, forcing her to her knees. With one hand he grabbed her hair and with the other he unbuckled his belt. The professor saw her distorted expression as her face was thrust with force. It's only a game for them...entertainment, he thought. He shot a burst of photos.

The Patient's voice came to him, strained and desperate. "We are not ready...I'm not ready for this so called advanced society, for its pettiness—the desires, the entertainment...all this seeking. It's selfish."

The Professor laughed. He didn't laugh at her, but at his own confusion as he watched the violent desire through his window. He had no answers. She was right. Nothing made sense.

Long ago, the Professor had discovered the woman's phone number. He would call, she would pick up the receiver and lay on her sofa, always naked in blue TV screen light, like a corpse. She never looked his way, but she knew he was watching. He enjoyed the power he felt. He revived her time after time.

Again, he dialed her number. His groin ached and he barely breathed, waiting.

The man in her flat held the receiver, his contorted, vile face glared at the Professor. "Watch this!" The man's voice shivered on the line. Insane. Violent. He wrapped the phone cord around her knees, threw her limp body over the couch and wedged the receiver between her thighs.

The Professor listened to sounds of wet flesh and the woman's cries, and his Patient's voice reeled on, "The people have no ideals! Is this freedom? Just look at the need to possess another human being. Is this what you call 'self-fulfillment' in your superior society?"

"And what does this mean in terms of your own marriage?" Startled by his own voice on the recording, the Professor's stomach wrenched. It was mockery. He mocked her!

"Everywhere marriage is failing. This is pure selfish individualism! It's not only commoners, but world leaders are drowning in domestic struggles. They lurch from one crisis to another until they see nothing in depth. They're incapable of seeing beyond their sphere of power!"

Truth is not possible here…perhaps only a relative truth, and a relative meaningfulness. To somehow feel connected to humanity was a craving that left him empty and unsatisfied. He could only stand at the window and watch. The man buckled his pants and fled the room. The woman bolted the door and stepped into the light of the moon. She stroked her arms and breasts as if to gather up her femaleness again, to feel that she was intact. The Professor felt her thoughts rise in a horrid scream and he felt as if her scream rose from his own gut.

He watched the woman retreat into the television's blue glare. If only he could hear her voice, if he could touch her tenderness, he might understand what his patient was saying. He would touch her and smooth away the deformities and lies of ordinary life. He would enter below the surface into her depths and maybe there, touch the principle truth of a new world coming, a not-so-concrete world, a not-so-moral and guilty world.

Again, the Patient's voice came to him, demanding, dragging him to the surface. Her sincerity mocked him. "How do we plan to establish order, to guarantee respect for human rights around the world? We are morally bankrupt. We no longer know why we are fighting, or what principles we defend."

It had been merely a voice, a scream. There had been nothing to connect it with. Night after night the scream delivered him into another zone, a place where he didn't recognize himself. Had he dreamed it each night? There was a hazy image, an obscure human form without shape, raising its sanctified arm in vain, against overwhelming injustice. It reminded him of his patient. He watched the woman lying there like a mannequin. She's an imitation, a reflection from the television perhaps, an illusion of a human being, but not the thing itself, not that which I long for.

"Our time is up." The tape clicked off.

He dialed the woman's number. It was human contact he needed, to feel the naked truth of facing her from his window. She lifted the receiver and let it fall. Her eyes met his without expression. The Professor shuddered and spasms of laughter took over. A nameless anxiety surrendered itself, releasing him from a lifetime of illusion. He took refuge in a vision of infinite perfection, of absolute truth. His eyes met hers. "Thank you," he whispered.

She watched as he raised his weapon. The Professor slumped to the floor, eyes fixed on the silence of night, and swallowed the scream.

FILMING PAVEMENT

Monique lives in the city with Jules. It is a shapeless city, or rather a city shaped by her dreams, where gleaming glass towers drift on an island between two oceans. The streets are rippling streams where her dreams run rampant and Jules films them. She's disappointed that Jules rarely films anything but feet. She thinks he's missing the point, but he says that he captures the formless that way. "Talking heads fill space with clutter," he said.

Monique thought he might be right. Her dreams were formless. Formless in the way that death can be, or perhaps, they are that way because Jules leaves out the forms. She'd lost track of whether her dreams are the subject of his art, or whether it's the other way around.

It all began on the morning that Jules filmed their legs. They were entwined from the waist down like a river flowing through their bed. Cat lay stretched at their feet, licking Monique's big toe. Jules smiled as he stroked her long, white neck and whispered, "I love you." He placed a small black box in her hands, then got up and walked out the door.

Monique could barely make out the letters that he'd scrawled on the box. *D-r-e-a-m*. It was a film clip. She slipped the film into a viewer and rolled onto her stomach. Cat walked on her back, kneading the flesh of her buttocks, then settled down, eyes closed, purring.

The clock ticked, missed a beat, then ticked again.

Monique watched closely. She saw Jules running down wet streets. She liked the smell of wet tar and wished she was the one exploring her dreams in the city. She wondered where he was.

The clock ticked, missed a beat, then ticked faster.

The camera jiggled and Monique saw a close up of Jules' green Keds with purple shoelaces. Monique smiled. She'd told him that people would think he was gay. He'd laughed at her and winked two winks, which meant, I only sleep with you, darl'n.

Monique saw a dog leash dragging on the ground. The leash was red with a silver cinch chain. Jule's camera focused on the leader of the leash, a rain-drenched white poodle with red booties. Monique gasped. There was no person in sight. The poodle was lost. It had a red bow in its curls, right between the ears. Monique knew this was a danger sign. Red meant danger. She'd remember to write that in her journal. She should never forget that.

Monique watched for clues. Where was the owner of the dog with the red booties? Ha! There! Jules found her, a thin lady with electric orange hair chased the poodle, frantic eyes open wide, her lips quivering, "My precious! Come back, my precious!" Hysterical sounds pooched out from her botched-Botox-lips where orange lipstick bled into cracks above her upper lip. Mascara ran in black streaks down her cheeks. Monique touched her own lips. She'd worn lipstick last night. Jules must have seen. He'd warned about dyed hair, Botox, and lipstick.

The clock ticked, missed a beat, then ticked slower.

The camera jiggled again. Another leash! She clicked her tongue. This one she knew. A green leash led to the hand of Darwin who was the owner of a smart dog, a gray and white Aussie Shepherd. She saw Darwin's boots. His feet moved quickly and with purpose. A glass door slid open as they approached a shop. Ah ha! Café de L'illusion. This was where Jules and Darwin met to study clues from her dreams. The video screen went black.

Monique closed her eyes and listened to the tick tock of the clock. Cat climbed on her tummy, stretched out and purred. She imagined that her hair was dyed orange and her lips painted red. She must wipe off the lipstick before Jules comes home because orange hair and lipstick stands for caution.

The clock ticked, missed a beat, two beats, three beats…ticked again…

Then Monique saw the red leash and the silver cinch chain. This meant that the thin lady didn't catch her dog. That's too bad. Now the dog was lost in a city of dream rivers. The lady must be lost too, without her little dog.

Monique rested her head on soft pillows, taking pleasure in Cat's warmth against her body. Behind her eyelids, the film continued to run. Ah! Someone is holding the leash. The strange lady found her dog. No! It's not the lady with her little dog. It was Jules' hand that held the leash.

The clock ticked, missed a beat, missed two beats...

Cat inched forward, crouching on Monique's chest, head stretched out, licking Monique's fingers, tasting her cold grip on the silver chain.

THE WOUND

Her limp cold body was full of loathing. For her I felt no remorse. In fact, it was a dog, a puppy that I felt for the most. The basement was enormous. Dirt floors worn to fine powder over a hundred years. Creaky wooden steps led from the kitchen to the basement. At the bottom was Father's wood shop where a small potbelly stove with tiny mica windows burned hot on winter nights. I sat at the top of the steps for hours, sometimes until three in the morning, inhaling wood dust and watching for fear he'd cut off his fingers at the table saw.

To the right of Father's workshop was a room full of antiques that my grandmother collected. In the next room, shovels and a pick ax hung neatly from wooden pegs just across from a concrete mud sink. Over this sink was a long board, skewered with steel hooks where my father hung rabbits to butcher. I would shut my eyes and gasp each time the iron rod snapped a rabbit's neck. This was a quick and painless death, my father said. What else had he killed? What would he kill? Visions of death came to me in my dreams.

From the mudroom, a darkened threshold led to the wine cellar, stacked high with father's homemade wine made from dark purple grapes. And in the middle of the wine cellar were stacks of burlap sacks packed with black walnuts. At Christmastime, our hands would stain black from shucking the green flesh. Mother cut the sacks into quarters and sewed pint-sized bags that we filled with gold-colored walnuts. The bags were tied with bright ribbons and we wrote names on small cards decorated with Santa and reindeer—Christmas gifts for our friends, along with freezer boxes packed with rabbit meat. The gaiety of Christmas prevailed over death. It was in this room filled with Christmas memories that I buried my mother. You must think that this is my confession but it's not. Just listen. One night I saw my mother in the mudroom with a puppy. It was a Dalmatian puppy, a Christmas gift from our grandmother. I crouched behind the door and watched while she tied the little dog to a wooden post in the middle of the room. As the mud sink filled with water the puppy turned to look at me, not afraid, only sad the same way I felt. The faucet creaked. The sink was full. We hadn't named the puppy and now it was too late. In that moment, I came to know the agony of hate. Any love I'd ever known was undone. She turned and walked into the wine cellar. I followed and watched as she began to dig. Through my tears, I saw myself bent over the hole, sobbing as I covered her face, as I covered her hands— hands that had held and caressed me, hands that had brushed my hair, hands that were now pale and cold like a childhood that never happened.

HOLY MAN

I am blind now for many years. Seventeen years to be exact. That is exactly, I tell you, the age of my son. I know what you are wondering. What has my life been like? I will tell you. I am worn down with so many regrets. Since my blindness, there is a constant breath in my ear, a dry rhythmic breath, so persistent that I walk and breathe to its haunting rhythm. My son leads me across a wooden footbridge toward the mountain path. He is strong and I am feeble. He learns at University and I fear for him because he is so proud. You understand? This is my torment. The distance between our worlds is like the endless space between two breaths. I could walk this path alone but for the danger of the black snake that lives on this mountain. It is called a 'five-stepper'. When the black snake strikes, you will walk five steps and fall dead. Most days I wish for this quick death. It will never come. My son will shoot the snake before it strikes. I am now seventy-eight years old. Fifty years ago, I was alone on the banks of this holy river. I wore no clothes. I sat in silence. Aloneness was my constant companion, my beloved. Today, I cry from this loss, racked with emptiness. But never mind. Are you really interested in my feelings? Or do you just want to stare at my nakedness, to have a story to tell of this crazy holy man that you met on the Ganges? Yes, do tell my story. You have my permission. As I was saying...the vision of her is a constant torment. She was tall and golden-haired. She was naked. I became hot with wanting. My body shook and I lost control of my senses. She came to me and showed me the other world. Her belly grew and she told me I must build a hut on the bank of the river. The boy was born and my joy was like the sun bursting inside of me. On that very day, the village elders came and pronounced a curse upon our lives. Since then I feel infested with worms. Worldly needs eat at my soul. Need is killing me. Do you see how we live now, burdened with endless duties? You foreigners come to our guesthouse. You come for teachings from this naked old man with a white flowing beard. Night after night I sit on my silk cushion while you sit on yours. Yes, my wife plays beautiful music and my son speaks seven languages. He recites lengthy scriptures from memory. You sit in awe. I sit in awe. My beloved has fled. Do you understand? Do you understand anything?

IMMORTAL ROOTS

There is always a yearning—
a powerful longing for freedom
from stern commandments
from fearful power
from meager answers.
My secret forest beckons me
resplendent, steaming world
sweetly fragrant, musty
with rotten stumps, fungus,
and colorful wet leaves.
I feel empowered, abundantly rich
possessed with a mouth, with nostrils and hands

with which to caress the world.

With purposeful strides

I enter the cool privacy

of my forest

treading the ground, my feet sprouting roots,

down into the Earth

seeking to mingle with those

who have gone beyond.

I'm an explorer in an exalted game

feeling sweetness and joy so great

that tears begin to flow

Ancient, mystical words rise up

from the rhythm of my footsteps

Eternal laws of Earth enter me

embroiled with life and death

Arriving at a clearing

I stand before my friend

an aged apple tree

bent and weathered like Lao Tzu

I climb, hopes raised

toward clear blue skies

chasm of hope

Inhaling the abyss

I wonder...

is the world only

my mind playing?

Does the Universe come from me?

Mind, heart and loins await a reply

from an unseen force

No answer comes

just a sudden fear of letting go

of falling

I swim in the ocean

of pain and suffering

reeking of desire

carnal pleasure and greed

desperate human cries arise

above the violent din of ambition

Sacrificing blood, spirit and soul

eyes clouded, obscuring grace

hearts paralyzed blind

my heart chokes with this

unbearable grip

pain consumes itself

leaving only ashes

of human dignity

an unexpected miracle...

compassion descends

leading me by the hand

through realms where

lingering rose scent and frankincense

linger

the beat of drums

soothes my heart

light bodies soar and hover

suffused with abundant soul

graceful, deathless elements

seep into every pore

healing lifetimes of suffering

again and again I

embrace the world

peering deeply into the chasm

between freedom and the sensual world

standing at the precipice

calm and tranquil

watching a play

of light and shadows

I see myself clearly

I am mother,

prostitute,

thief, rogue

and monk.

The question has baked in a blazing fire

half a lifetime

now the answer

is no longer important,

mind can be so vain

so dangerous

Don't you see, O' hapless child

The Universe simply IS~

INDIA

MILLIONS OF FINE THREADS WEAVE THE paradox that is India. These are my traveling stories. Not facts and figures about tourist attractions, but my personal stories, my connection with the people of India. At the time of these writings I'd landed on the Asian continent for the third time. And for the third time I had no idea why I was going around the world to be extremely uncomfortable. Nonetheless, I was drawn to India in a powerful way. India felt profoundly familiar.

FOUR LITTLE BOYS,
TSUNAMIS & POLITICS

There they are, all brown-skinned buns cozy in the sand, four little penises pointing to the sun—so innocent, expecting nothing and everything on the shore of the Arabian Sea.

Indians have a way of moving. They glide, ethereal-like, as if the earth carried them, lifting them from one place to another. Think how it feels to walk on moving walkways at the airport. It's easy, almost effortless. The Indian way of moving has this ease. The other extraordinary way-ness of Indians is their born-in self-confidence. Not learned, not affected. Beggar, taxi driver, cushion salesman or priest, all seem to flow with time through the days, the hours, the minutes—as if they owned earth, fire, water, and air. As if they were themselves these things. Okay, maybe not all Indians. But even the rickshaw drivers, arguing over a fare, threatening each other with a slap of a chappal, even these screaming Indians are embraced by a gentle wind.

What makes me think of this is the way the waves lift me

and set me down. In these foreign waters I'm buoyant… beyond buoyant, and the water is softer than the finest Pashmina. It holds me like I've never been held. Not by any man. Not by any woman. It is unconditional. It could kill me, but that too would be unconditional.

Tonight, a soft rain trickles through the palm fronds, a '40s love song plays somewhere in the darkness and the baby downstairs begins to cry. Only the sea is constant, breathing in and out, not knowing how it will rock us to sleep in time. Just not knowing.

The so-special sub worlds of all of us will disappear into the night, into the sleep. Ever wonder where we go in our sleep? We are here and then we are not here, and then out of nowhere, we are here again. Like a tsunami. I think about tsunamis when I'm out in the waves, looking back toward the beach. Someone would see it coming and scream. In that moment, our so-special-separate-lives would crash into each other, a mass of fear running from a force of nature. But where do we run? At least to the far side of that dike of boulders that stands like a fortress between sea and coconut palms. Would it be futile to tie ourselves to a palm tree with a beach cloth? Maybe we could tie ourselves together in a chain? How much time do we have?

Never mind I tell myself, this isn't going to happen today and for God sake, there are more urgent things to worry about…like the rule of the land…how our lives will never be the same again. We may feel a reluctant nudge and ask: Is this really happening? Again? Do we have a choice?

A BEGGAR AND A DOG

Beggars, hundreds of beggars, lean into the street with outstretched hands. I stop to watch a well-doer offer a biscuit to one skin-and-bones man. These exchanges intrigue me. This beggar accepts the biscuit, but with some reticence. It's clear that he prefers coins, and I can understand that. Absolutely. If he has coins, he can buy what he wants and he doesn't have to eat vanilla biscuits if he prefers ginger biscuits. The beggar was less than grateful. Now, the well-meaning biscuit donor walks away wondering what he did wrong. Just then up walks a skin-and-bones dog sniffing around the beggar. The beggar offers the biscuit to the dog but the dog takes one sniff and saunters away. Now the beggar is miffed and starts throwing pieces of broken biscuit after the dog while yelling insults…*Tairiyam*! The audacity!

The beggar grins at me as he looks up and points to the full moon that shines over the holy mountain known as Arunachala.

SACRED COW

Recently, I was traveling just to see what was sane and what was insane in the rest of the world. I happened upon the musky backwaters of South India. It wasn't easy walking along the narrow paths, wet with monsoon rains and the dung of oxen that spattered my linens. Overhead, ripe coconuts threatened to drop. Ahead of me marched barefoot village men wearing ragged cotton dhotis to cover the necessary. Civil war vintage muskets and ammo belts were slung across their bony shoulders. There's no point in making sense of these things.

The atmosphere was hypnotic in a lazy day sort of way. An orange sun played shadow tricks over the water, turning innocent branches into snakes. At the edge of a field, far too close for comfort, a massive bull mounted a pure white cow, her horns brightly painted and decorated with garlands of red carnations, her eyes bulging with fear. I stood mesmerized by the sight, by the insistent animal thrusts, by the shocking grandness of it all.

As luck would have it, God was watching just then, and God saw two young women, one white-skinned woman with golden hair and one brown-skinned woman with coconut-oiled black hair. God saw that the two women thought they were alone. And God also saw that the two women were breathing hard, that their blood pulsed hot in their veins and rose to color their faces. God felt the tension in the air and wondered at the unseen force that bridled this passion. God did not intervene.

NO TIME ZONE THIS OCEAN

Constant waves all day long, all night long, wrap around me, turn me over, and spin me into a cocoon of silence. There's extraordinary intimacy inside my cocoon, with feelers that reach out and touch things, to sense and to share all that cannot be spoken.

I'm at a beach resort in South India on the shore of the Arabian Sea. Three women, one German, one American, and one Italian and her husband. None of us speaks the others' language. All three women are reading the same book. Our three copies lay on identical bamboo tables in front of identical rooms. We three notice this and nod, giving a thumbs up and smile — a silent camaraderie. All three women have the same cough, the same burning in the lungs, the same complaint about diesel fumes and burning plastic in the places we came from. All three women were visiting ashrams, but three different ashrams. Now, we transcend any illusion of purity and happily treat our mutual bronchitis with codeine-laced cough syrup.

This, the Italian husband (our man on deck, you could say) picked up at the local pharmacy. "So, I can get some sleep!" he pantomimes.

The Italian husband was nearly killed one day as he relaxed in a hammock. A coconut crashed from thirty feet above and just missed his head. We all saw it happen. Or, rather, not happen. Death postponed.

This incident mobilized the children of the neighborhood. They appeared out of nowhere, and lacking the usual tool, a sickle for opening a ripe coconut, they devised their own method. The girls set out to maneuver the coconut into a strategic and balanced placement on a large rock. They stepped back and turned sideways to avoid shrapnel as the boys took turns heaving a large rock upon the head of the coconut. Each unsuccessful attempt is followed by a re-maneuver of the coconut by the girls. In the end, the coconut is shattered and the children scrape out the meat with bits of broken rock. They know we are watching, as tourists do, and look up at us, smiling and holding up their prize.

MARTINIS, LIMES & PUBERTY

Today my lunch is a complex concoction of diced fresh tomato slathered in HAPPY brand Lime Pickle sauce. I made it myself. I'm happy and the pickle jar is happy back.

The HAPPY brand logo boasts a dwarf-sized Mickey Mouse wearing a red jumper and red top hat. Mickey is cheering his way to happiness, holding high a martini glass. I never thought of pairing gin with Lime Pickle Sauce, but well…there must be something in that sauce as I'm sitting here writing about such a thing.

The color of HAPPY lime pickle sauce reminds me of blood. Naturally, my mind leaps to puberty…of course! there must be a rite of passage in India that involves limes. And so there is. If I had been born in India, into a certain sect of Hinduism, my entire family would be involved in my first blood flow. I'm now in a state of 'ritual pollution' and I'm in for a cleansing that will be performed by all my aunts and blood cousins on my father's side. This is a two-week process during which time I am fed an elaborate cleansing diet of assorted fruits dressed with ginger oil, raw turmeric, and coconut. My aunts bathe me in specially prepared water imbued with turmeric powder, seven types of flowers and three limes. Exactly three limes.

After the final turmeric bath, all my aunts and blood cousins dress me for my Puberty Ceremony. I wear a silk sari, shiny jewels and garlands of jasmine. I am now fit to be blessed. A brass lamp is filled with ghee, the wicks are lit and the ceremony begins. My condition is announced to the entire family. My mother's brothers (my uncles) have first choice of winning me as a bride, and I have one opportunity to say 'PASS'.

Even though I'm a 'modern' Indian woman, I indulge in the wishes of my elders and understand that the value of this ritual is the space it creates for intimacy with my women people. Cloistered with my mother, my aunts and cousins, my 'Book of Predications' is opened. At birth, certain astrological data was entered. I was born on a Thursday at 4:30 am. It is written that this is a good omen, bidding fairness and a virtuous life. As I'm just fifteen years old, this remains to be seen. There is time.

WHAT EXACTLY IS A
SPIRITUAL PRACTICE?

Honest, I learned what meditation is while riding a motorbike in India. There's really no choice but to let go to stay alive. That is, to let go of any concept of what is right and what is wrong on the road to anywhere. To let go of any rules, especially about obeying road signs. Why bother to honk your horn when everyone is honking at once. Or, why *not* honk your horn?

When in India, I often ride a motorbike to explore rural areas and navigate the city streets. This is no small feat—to survive the homicidal confusion of roads where there is left side driving but where vehicles pass on the right and the left, where speeding buses and lorry trucks loaded with granite rocks barrel down roads, demanding the right-of-way. Near death experiences are common, some more memorable than others.

Monsoon rains have made a mess of the roads and I'm on a mission to deliver medicine for a sick child in a remote village. Through a maze of tuk tuks, pedestrians and cows, a rambling bullock cart sways up the middle of the road, loaded with bundles of rebar that spans from ditch to ditch. Horns blare, traffic swerves and cows meander on as usual. Braking vehicles throw clouds of dust in the air and small stones pummel my face. The dire-ness of this absurdity I comprehend in the nick of time. I close my eyes and duck. Closing my eyes is a reflex that makes no sense at all, but decapitation seemed a real possibility and I didn't want to see it happen. My cheek pressed to the gas tank, I feel the hard steel of rebar skim over my back. A second later I'm surprised to find my body intact. But here is the mind-bender. Ahead, a yellow triangle looms ahead, warning of danger. Decorated with a black skull and bones the sign reads:

CONGESTED TRAFFIC

SORRY FOR THE INCONVENIENCE

It's a matter of physics that I apply to the Indian system of driving—a harmony of the infinitesimal where energy and matter move like fluids. But alas, I have only one gear and a rear brake that I confuse with the horn. By the grace of all the Gods, I survive.

Continuing my journey, I venture down a narrow road that ends at the edge of a swamp. It's not long after setting off on foot that I meet another obstacle, this one more difficult. Blocking my path are two cows, decorated with brightly painted horns and brass bells. The cow on my left is urinating a stream in my pathway and the cow on my right is shitting in the wet stream of the other. Looking down at my new sandals and spattered Punjabi, I laugh. After all, on this day, I've been given another round in life. Cow shit is nothing.

EMPEROR MING HUANG'S HORSE

There's a famous Chinese drawing in the I Ching of a horse named Cheo-ye-po. He's shown tethered to a tree in the forest, rearing up and neighing frantically. He wants to run but can't.

I'm like Cheo-ye-po and rear up with a well-founded cynicism. Welcome to my past. It was 1981 when I first set foot in India and met a living guru. To be here now is to re-visit 'beginners mind'. Indeed, India will strip you of any sense of self that is imagined, cultivated, or dreamed. You become lost in chaotic sights, smells, and sounds, in the infuriating illogical sensibilities of Indian ways. You turn around, looking for your familiar self and find nothing there. Not in your surroundings and not in your mind.

Ashrams are places that claim not to be a *religious organization*, but cultivate the trappings of a religious organization, where the seriously pure find smiles frivolous—places where newcomers are numbed beyond reason by an idealistic seeking for something they will never find. On the upside, there's diversity. Muslim and Hindu, Jewish, Christian and Catholic, Atheists and Agnostics—all are here in this Hindu ashram for a Yoga retreat.

The struggle to remain separate is Cheo-ye-po's problem. And mine. I've come to this ashram to revive a flailing yoga practice. Standing on my head twice a day shakes down my resistance and I let go to the 'now'. But not totally. The first days are a nightmare. I resist every social convention of ashram life, but it's not long before I meet kindred spirits, fellow rule breakers. We skip the insufferable chanting and opt for a swim at the lake. Another day we go out to the village coffee stand and meet a few orange-clad ashram swamis ducking out for coffee and pastries. Listening and watching has its reward. I resist less and appreciate more.

What is it about ashram life that's different from anywhere else? Same Same But Different says one T-shirt walking next to a Spiritual Gangster T-shirt.

Once I'm stripped down of my concepts and no longer neighing and tugging, then what? Well, there's still the herd behavior to survive. In the whirlwind of ashram life, those that follow instructions tend to snub those that don't. But it all ends in a wash. No one changes anyone else. What does happen (more or less) is that we let go of thinking that anyone should change. Now, when our stripped-down-selves brush past each other on the ashram path, we recognize one another in that ever-so-precious way. This I cannot bear...this preciousness engendered by ashram life among co-seekers on the path to enlightenment. Who do we think we are?

But then I remember, that yoga practice is all about surrender. The subtle Grace we sense on this common ground may be imagined or it may be real, but what does matter if the 'seriously pure' are now smiling?

DIGITAL SOUL

Where am I? It's an ashram-y sort of place but more like a university. Like many ashrams, after the founding guru dies, this one too must fend for itself. It is small, intimate, and raucous. Yogis and yoginis chat up a storm in twelve languages. Women wear t-shirts stretched across real and fake bosoms boasting their status as 'Spiritual Gangster' or 'Digital Soul.'

Indeed. At break time, the meditation hall of white marble and elegant pillars is occupied by truth-seekers typing on mini laptops, connected globally by Facebook and Skype. Gone are the days of colorfully clad lovers of God dancing ecstatic in the temple.

What is typical Indian fashion are the sleeping quarters for these yogis in training. These are thatch-covered rooftops where mosquito nets dangle over a multitude of very thin mattresses on weathered cement. The toilet is half a mile away, down a flight of steep steps.

On the first morning of my stay at this particular ashram, I wake to the sound of vigorous rhythmic grunts, followed by long guttural groans. Human-like sounds, but deeper throated. Primal sounds. This can't be, I think…not in the ashram where such behavior is forbidden. Later I learn that these sounds of ecstasy come from lions in heat. Lions that live across the lake, contained by a mere twenty-foot chain-link fence.

During the past month, I've done more Surya Namaskar than in my entire life. This yoga routine is brutal at a fast pace. You've seen it—hands pressed together in Namaste, Salute the sun god! Fingertips stretch toward the skies then plummet to the ground while thrusting legs out from under. Your chest skims the floor, and then you hold the length of your body parallel just inches above the floor, and so on. At home in California our yoga wallahs guide us through these moves in gentle, nurturing voices while pleasant music plays from surround sound. But here…you'd think the coaches were trained by the military.

"Hutt! Inhale. Chest up! Back straight! Hutt Hutt! Exhaaaale. Relaaaax."

I've never sweated so much and I've never felt better in my life. Served only two bland meals a day, no coffee, no meat, no wine, and four hours of intense yoga each day, I've never slept better.

Outside the ashram, soft hills surround a large lake. Exotic flute sounds drift through the early morning mist. Peacocks and macaws call. I step outside the ashram gates for a bit of peace and quiet. Paradox is India.

SAME SAME BUT DIFFERENT

It does seem that my 'inner fire' burns hotter in this place. There is a sacred mountain that is believed to be the embodiment of Shiva himself. Arunachala looms over the village, looking upon a chaotic mix of Indian and Western absurdities. There's a playful atmosphere among the co-seekers that gather here. We are all playing a game. A game of the mind. A game of searching for something that can never be found.

What is this 'thing' that can never be found? An esteemed pundit beams a benevolent smile and points toward the heavens, "You are already 'That.' For this reason, you cannot search for that which you already are."

Many come to sit in this energy, to hear this over and over with the vague notion that they will have a direct experience of 'enlightenment'. But the esteemed pundit is not exactly right.

Another seeker of truth, Sri Ramana Maharshi wrote of his experience that led to the desired state of unchanging awareness. He was sixteen years old when a violent fear of death drove his mind inward. He described a direct perception of the omnipresent 'Self' that occurred as a vivid flash of insight, without any thought process. After this insight, Ramana Maharshi wrote:

"...the usual thoughts come and go but the 'I' (or Self) continues unbroken, like the various notes of music, like the fundamental musical note that underlies and blends with all other notes."

As I write this, I can say that I'm definitely not having this experience. Nevertheless, there is hope. Recently, a friend explained that only by 'searching' can we come to the realization that enlightenment cannot be found by searching, like the story of someone who travels around the world in search of a treasure which he finally discovers in his own back yard.

ONE HOUR TO PARADISE

IndiGo air carries me from South East India to South West India in one hour. I'm headed to Kerala, the most literate of India's thirty-six states, boasting 99% literacy. On board, the flight attendant reminds me of myself in the sixth grade. She wears an auburn pixie-styled wig and navy blue opaque pantyhose beneath a tight skirt with a kick pleat center back.

So, how does one become an IndiGo flight attendant? It says right here on the back of the menu card. The recruiting statement invites application by "young women between the age of 18 and 23 who want to live a jet-set lifestyle, receive a high salary, and wear designer uniforms. You must be 172.72 centimeters' tall minimum, and the body must be pleasantly proportionate with this height and have a clear complexion."

What do I think? I think it's a good job if you can get it.

I turn my attention to the late 50-ish, Indian man

sitting next to me and find that he's a physicist working for the Indian government on National Defense. We don't talk about India's defense plans, but about the two-party government system of Kerala State. Currently, the Communist Party is in office. The other party is the 'Congress', which is the democratic faction. Apparently, the power shifts between these two parties every four years when the people are fed up with whichever party they elected the previous term. According to my seatmate, this back and forth strategy seems to work. The Communist Party pours money into social systems for the people, allocating the minimum for improvements of the infrastructure or government worker wages. The next term, the Congress Party gets its chance to bleed money from the social programs in order to improve roads and city plumbing, while paying themselves a hefty salary. When the people feel the pain of this, they rally to bring back the Communists. The two-party system works because among the three factions of Keralite society—Christian, Hindu and Muslim, there is no majority. Very simply put, these factions "live and let live." A simplistic view I'm sure, but there you have it.

One hour later I'm off the plane and in a taxi. The roads are much better here than in Tamil Nadu, but still, I'm uncomfortable with headlights coming straight at the car I'm riding in. It doesn't help to see signs with skull and bones posted every kilometer that reads:

ACCIDENT PRONE ZONE.

AVOCADOS AND DESIGNER SMILES

Indians are graced with subtle ways and mannerisms that are unique, even charming if you tend to be a glass-half-full sort of person rather than a glass-half-empty sort of person.

Entering a restaurant for example, you are greeted by a line-up of unsmiling faces. Not unfriendly, and not overly friendly. An elegant wave of the hand bids you, "sit." Or maybe, "please sit." Your waiter then saunters away leaving you to find a seat for yourself.

Perhaps half an hour or so later you look around for the waiter. As if on cue, he turns toward you, as if woken from a standing-up nap.

He rushes over. "Yes madam, what do you want?"

Or, alternatively, the waiter will stand in front of you and say nothing, his gaze fixed on a distant place, waiting for you to assert yourself.

On one such occasion, I say: "Hel-llo… may I please see a menu?"

"You like menu?"

Now, I'm not a naturally mean-hearted person, but if pressed, I can be. This is a sign of the fire in some Sagittarians. So, I'll say something like,

"That would be nice…maybe sometime today." (with a slight twist and jab action on *sometime*), and a phony smile.

The menu appears after I've had time to wonder if he's forgotten that I'm there. Experienced travelers bring a good book or smoke half a pack of Garam Clove cigarettes while enjoying the view. These are fascinating hours of the day and should be cherished. After all, this is India. No hurry, no worries.

Today, in a funky beach restaurant, I order an avocado sandwich. Happily, I wait, watching the waves roll in and out and watching other people watch the waves roll in and out.

An ant on the table catches my attention, so I slip a shiny card out from under the red plastic ashtray filled with Garam butts, and use the card to whisk the ant out of my sight. Having accomplished that, I take a good look at the card—bright pink print on a pea green background. It reads:

Dr. Shukkoor's Dental Spa

A Multi-Specialty Clinic

"We Design Your Smile"

I turn the card over, examining both sides a couple of times. There's a quote here by Dr. Shukkoor himself:

"There is no such part in human body that demands such a judicious mix of functionality & creativity as the teeth."

So entertained, I hardly notice the passing time, except that the sun has moved a good deal farther west since I sat down. Timidly, I interrupt the waiter who appears to be hypnotized by a baby gecko trapped inside a red Chinese lantern.

He rushes to my table. "Yes Madam?"

"Avocado sandwich is coming?" I ask.

"Avocado is not ready Madam, maybe tomorrow, maybe next day. You like chips, maybe fruit?"

The waiter smiles and I can't help but wonder if this young man is getting a big kick out of it all. But then, maybe I'm just paranoid and should give him the benefit of the doubt.

I smile back, pick up my things to leave, trying to not let my pissed-off-ness show. "Oh, no problem."

With a benevolent smile and charming head wag as if he'd just served a first-rate meal and gotten a generous tip, he bids me well. "Yes, Madam, no problem…see you tomorrow."

ABBA'S INTERNET

ABBA is a café on north cliff in Varkala, boasting a comprehensive menu—serving Thai, Chinese, Italian, English, Israeli, Nepalese, and, last but not least, Indian and "all manner of fresh seafood" ALL ORGANIC AND LOCAL GROWN. It says so right here on the menu.

ABBA has a cunning way of serving up the Internet. Granted, it's free.

"No charge, Madam."

"Super! And the password is?"

My inquiry is met with blank stares from three handsome Nepalese boys. I realize that I need a different word. I need their word for 'password' and I need that they don't shuffle away before I get it. Life has become desperate and it's not yet 8 a.m. The Globetrotter Internet connection (Guaranteed High Speed) at my accommodation is a non-happening.

I look around at the rain-stained walls and for some reason 'Davinci' comes to mind, and by the magic of free association, by God, I've got it! CODE.

I catch their attention: "Code? What is the Code?"

Their faces brighten.

"Ah, you want Code?"

"Yes, that would be super."

The boys all understand 'Super!' which means that I'm happy. This makes them want to please me and these beautiful young men try hard to help me understand.

"Madam, we change each four hours the Code"

"Good idea," I say: "So, what is the code this hour?"

"What is the hour, madam?"

The young men wait patiently while I fetch my phone to find the hour.

"The hour, baba, is fifteen before 8:00 am."

 I'm rewarded with smiles all around and I feel triumphant.

"Madam, the Code now is…please wait…"

I wait and no one says anything. There is a quick exchange between them, a slight smile? Do I detect a bit of mirth? All three walk away.

"Wait wait!"

One of them turns back, "No Madam, please wait."

Finally, an eavesdropping Brit, says: "The code is 'please wait'…all one word."

"Ah, thank you very much!"

Over the next days, we go through a similar routine. One day at noon the Code is "8 by 8" which comes around to eight 8's. One of the boys traces it on the tabletop. On the next shift, I hear "eight eights" and try for several minutes typing in eight eights with no success. I ask again.

"No, no Madam." He traces the letter 'a' on the tabletop and taps 8 times, smiling sweetly: "Code is eight ayes… small ayes." He shows me that the eight ayes are lower case by holding his thumb and index finger close together.

"Super!"

"You happy?"

"Yes, happy!"

"Enjoy beautiful day," he says.

'OPPORCHOONTY' IS HERE

G-string clad tourists lay sprawled in the sand, working on their tans, reading, watching fishermen work. But what's this? The fishermen wave vigorously, "Come, come! Help us, help us! Yes, come help!"

Beach bathers slowly bring the scene into focus, peering through their Ray-Bans and Maui Jims at the sun-wrinkled fisherman who smile broadly, flashing their betel-stained teeth. They're inviting the lounging tourists to join them as the catch is ready to be hauled to shore. The fishermen chant louder as pale young men rise to the occasion. The young men are hesitant and look to see if they are but a lone fool drawn to this venture.

I watch from my safe place against the stone dike, enjoying a clove cigarette. The first responder reminds me of Apostle James, thin with limp blond hair and a sparse beard, looking full of purpose. The fishermen are clearly amused and with great gladness, make room for volunteers.

"Heave-ho!" The pulling begins. As the rope reels in the catch, an ancient fisherman with one arm coils the rope neatly on the sand. As it goes, the last person on the rope moves to the front of the line with each coiling. No one is at the back more than one minute. The rotation is constant and the pulling is hard. Our white boys check out the damage, shaking their hands, rubbing their calves. Some run back to their beach blanket and grab a shirt to protect their hands from chaffing.

This goes on for nearly an hour. Some of the boys drop out, heads hanging. Apostle James hangs in, driven by who knows what. Finally, the net is in and the fishermen huddle around to assess the catch. Today it's Sardines. Buyers appear, scrambling over the dike, dressed in polyester pants with faux leather belts and shiny shirts with pointy collars. The haggling begins and all present shout, shove, spit and gesture with passion. The fishermen and the buyers seem not to agree on which buyer gets the goods and for how much money. Fists full of rupees are waved overhead, even thrown on the ground, at which point, old women in ragged saris show up out of nowhere, scrambling for the money. Later, these women will carry the fish in huge aluminum tubs balanced on their heads to the marketplace. The volunteer boys retreat to their beach blankets, examine their wounds and watch videos of themselves in action. Girlfriends smile proudly.

ECHO

"Psst! You there, under the Neem tree… Come sit. I have a secret to tell you."

"Whose secret?"

"You will know, though not just yet. Once not so long ago, a girl like yourself tripped over these tree roots and bled from a wound. She grimaced, reached up and tore a branch of Neem to stop the bleeding. It was then that a dream was born."

"Does the dream come true?"

"That is for you to decide my friend. I will tell you how it began. It was a long time ago and she was still a child, but nearly old enough to be married. She sat cross-legged on the dirt floor of her village hut, cleaning rice for the family dinner. Her mother lit a few dry branches under a pot of water. Just as the fire crackled, the sound of temple bells echoed across the village. It was then that the girl heard the voice for the first time. The voice, very close and hollow, dared her to leave her task, to step on the jungle path and run away.

"The girl did not look back as she left the hut. She knew that she would never return to this place where her family dwelt. The girl did not know her way to the famous temple where she'd heard about young girls who danced in the Inner Sanctum. She followed an overgrown path through fields of sugar cane. Parakeets, cuckoos and mynahs cawed and screeched. The sweet scent of fertile earth mingled with river smells and incense, guiding her on the path. Just as the sun dipped low, the largest temple in all India came into view, soaring brilliant against a deep blue sky. Discordant temple bells rang and the bellowing conch surged through her body. She'd barely caught her breath when she came upon the temple courtyard.

"'Hello please! Paisa! Paisa! Hello! Hello!'

"Small children tugged at the sleeves of tourists and begged in shrill voices. Flower sellers peered at her through brightly colored veils and the girl wondered if she would escape such a life. She was but a poor village girl and already promised for marriage. The girl pushed through the crowds, slipping off her sandals at the temple door. Worshipers rushed her along the corridors that led to the Inner Sanctum. Her heart pounded as she entered. The girl bowed before the Shiva Lingam and offered a garland of carnations, and a prayer:

"'Lord Shiva, God of Creation and Sustenance, accept me into your Temple. I offer myself in your service.'

"Temple Dancers smoothed their costumes, preparing to dance. Their skin shone with sandalwood paste and sweet smelling oil.

The tal of drum sounded…takataka da-da tika taka da. "Dancers tapped their toes, poised to begin. Now, understand, my dear…the young girl was shy. Dancers whirled around the Lingam, their faces lit by the fire. She watched and was overcome with a desire she'd never known, an unbearable longing. Bare feet slapped the stone floor to the rhythm of her pulse. She rose to join the dancers. Her body throbbed, opening to a sublime drunkenness. Her spirit soared with ecstasy, her soul swept upward—she was gone, exploding in the light!"

"Then what happened?"

"Ah…one day you will know, when it is time. You, who wish to dance, remember that I am always here in the echo of temple bells. I am your very own breath. Listen my friend, and you will hear eternity."

ee cummings wrote: "pleasure and pain are merely surfaces…love makes the little thickness of the coin…"

When we see an expression in a friend's eye and know the meaning; when we hear forgiveness in a sigh; when we watch a small kindness that makes us smile; or we ache inside for another's loss—in these small things there is a glimpse of our common humanness, and this is extraordinary.

DANA MACY studied East-West Cultural Studies at California Institute of Integral Studies (CIIS) in San Francisco. She lives in Ojai, California with her partner, a little monster of a cat and a sweet Rottweiler.

About the cover Type

Nakata is a hand drawn font and was published by Hanoded Nakata. OpenType features include Contextual Alternates and Standard Ligatures with extensive Latin language support.

www.ingramcontent.com/pod-product-compliance
Lightning Source LLC
Chambersburg PA
CBHW070334130626
46556CB00007B/2860